Rubbed the wrong way

by Aurealia Nelson

ISBN 979-8-89686-648-0

ISBN 979-8-89686-648-0

9 798896 866480

Staten House

Dedication

To all the mildly grumpy genies out there, struggling to maintain their composure in a world of utterly baffling humans. May your tea always be perfectly brewed (and not volcanically erupted), and may your wishes (however poorly articulated) occasionally come true.

This one's for you. And also, a special shout-out to my incredibly patient editor who managed to decipher my increasingly incoherent scribbles throughout the writing of this book. You're a saint (or perhaps, a particularly understanding genie in disguise). We both know it could have been worse. Much, much worse. I shudder to imagine the alternative... a book filled with nothing but sentient teacups arguing about the merits of Earl Grey versus Darjeeling. The horror! The sheer, unadulterated HORROR! Thank you, thank you, a thousand times thank you. You saved us all.

Preface

Let me be clear: this is not your typical genie story. Forget shimmering palaces, bountiful feasts, and wishes granted with effortless grace. This is the story of Azrael, a genie whose magic is about as reliable as a three-legged stool on a trampoline, and whose patience is thinner than a politician's promises. Expect chaos, expect incompetence, and expect a healthy dose of witty sarcasm, delivered straight from the perpetually exasperated perspective of our lead character. I've attempted to capture the essence of a truly awful day, amplified tenfold by the addition of poorly executed magic, clueless humans, and a persistent flock of philosophy-loving pigeons. Prepare yourself for a rollercoaster of absurdity, laced with enough relatable frustration to make even the most stoic reader crack a smile. And if, by some miracle, you manage to finish this without experiencing at least a mild sense of secondhand embarrassment for Azrael (and the humans he encounters), well, then congratulations. You have a higher level of tolerance for human folly than I possess.

Introduction

Welcome, dear reader, to the mildly chaotic life of Azrael. As you are about to discover, being a genie isn't all it's cracked up to be, especially when your magic malfunctions more often than it works, and your clientele consists primarily of teenagers with unrealistic expectations, clueless magicians, forgetful librarians, and a self-help guru whose positive affirmations have the opposite of their intended effect. This is a story of escalating absurdity, where a simple wish for a cup of tea can trigger a minor volcanic eruption, reality TV crews mistake you for a hairy extra, and philosophical pigeons hold you hostage for gourmet cheese. Azrael's journey is one of increasing frustration, punctuated by moments of surprisingly relatable exasperation. Get ready to witness the comedic collision of fantastical elements and the everyday absurdities of modern life, all viewed through the perpetually grumpy lens of a genie who might just consider retirement, preferably in a dimension far, far away from any human interaction whatsoever. But for now, let's dive into the wonderfully weird world of Azrael, and see if his day can possibly get any worse (spoiler alert: it does).

The Insistent Teenager

The insistent chirping of a particularly obnoxious alarm clock – a plastic flamingo that inexplicably sang off-key versions of Gregorian chants – jolted Azrael awake. He groaned, a sound somewhere between a rusty hinge and a dying walrus. Another day, another barrage of poorly-considered wishes from humanity's less-than-brightest specimens. This time, the culprit was already in full swing.

"More wishes! Come on, genie-man! I've run out of wishes!" a high-pitched voice screeched from somewhere near his makeshift bed (a surprisingly comfortable pile of discarded laundry).

Azrael peeled open one eye, the other stubbornly refusing to cooperate. The source of the noise was a teenager, sprawled across his "bed," clad in mismatched pajamas and sporting a truly impressive collection of brightly coloured hair clips. The teenager clutched a well-worn, glitter-encrusted copy of "1001 Genie Wishes You'll Never Believe Are Possible!"

"Young man," Azrael grumbled, his voice raspy from a particularly long nap fueled by residual magical exhaustion, "Clause 3b of the standard genie contract clearly states that wishes are not, in fact, unlimited. Three wishes, as per the agreement. Three. We went over this yesterday."

The teenager, apparently oblivious to the concept of legal agreements or basic numeracy, waved a dismissive hand. "But...but the book says...!"

Azrael sighed, a sound like a punctured tire. He'd encountered countless individuals who'd misinterpreted the ancient texts, but this teenager was on a whole new level of miscomprehension. He looked less like someone who'd read the fine print and more like someone who'd used the fine print as confetti.

"The book is fiction, my dear boy," Azrael explained, his patience already wearing thin. "It's a novel designed to sell more copies, not a guide to reality. A highly inaccurate one at that. Think of it as...

highly creative, interpretative dance on the subject of wishes."

"But I want a pony! A flying pony! And a lifetime supply of pizza rolls! And also... a solid gold skateboard! And...," the teenager continued, launching into a list of increasingly extravagant and nonsensical desires. Each request was delivered with the unwavering certainty of someone who'd just discovered the ultimate cheat code to life.

Azrael attempted subtle guidance, the preferred method for dealing with these situations. "Perhaps," he suggested, "a smaller, more manageable pony? Perhaps one that doesn't fly? Or maybe... a slightly less calorific alternative to pizza rolls? Perhaps... broccoli? Nutritious, you see..."

This suggestion, however, was completely lost on the teenager. He had apparently moved on to the next item on his wish-list which included an army of miniature robots programmed to do his homework and a self-cleaning bedroom. His enthusiasm was only matched by his utter lack of awareness of the impending reality of a mildly grumpy genie with limited magical reserves.

Azrael knew this wasn't going to end well. His magic was already sputtering, weakened by his less-than-ideal diet consisting mainly of dust bunnies and the occasional forgotten biscuit. This teenager's insatiable appetite for wishes was akin to setting off a chain reaction in a poorly-maintained magical reactor.

The first sign of magical malfunction was subtle, a slight shimmer in the air, barely noticeable. Then it escalated. The teenager's request for a solid gold skateboard caused a minor tremor that shook the dusty attic. His demand for a self-cleaning bedroom resulted in a miniature tornado that swept through the room, depositing a pile of strangely organized socks in the center of the chaos.

"Look at it! It's working!" the teenager shrieked, seemingly oblivious to the destruction unfolding around him. "This is awesome!"

Azrael, meanwhile, was frantically trying to regain control, his brow furrowed in concentration. The reality was that a request for a lifetime supply of pizza rolls was about to plunge him into a state of magical exhaustion that would last until the next millennium. The ensuing chaos wouldn't just be limited to his current location. It would spread across cities, possibly countries. If he was lucky. A catastrophic magical meltdown was looming. The sheer volume of sugar in those rolls was likely to cause some very serious problems on a cosmic scale.

He tried a different approach. "Perhaps," he said, his voice strained, "we could focus on one wish at a time? A small, achievable wish? Something... modest?"

The teenager considered this, tapping his chin thoughtfully. "Okay," he conceded, "but make it a really, really good wish." He paused, a mischievous glint in his eyes. "I wish for..."

Azrael braced himself. He had a feeling this "really good wish" was about to be something completely out of his magical league, something to rival the Great Magical Calamity of 1487 and the infamous incident with the singing toasters of 2023. He closed his eyes, waiting for the inevitable. He wasn't ready to face another day of magical mishaps but if he had to, at least he'd be prepared for whatever madness his current situation would deliver. He had a feeling it would involve copious amounts of cheese, and perhaps a small war between sentient squirrels and a very angry badger.

The Misunderstood Magic

The teenager, a lanky creature named Kevin with a questionable fashion sense involving mismatched socks and a shirt featuring a cartoon unicorn riding a skateboard, bounced on the balls of his feet, practically vibrating with anticipation. "So," Kevin chirped, his voice echoing oddly in the cramped kitchen, "the really good wish?"

Azrael sighed, a sound like air leaking from a punctured magic carpet. He rubbed his temples, feeling the familiar throb of a magical headache brewing. His usual iridescent blue skin had taken on a distinctly greenish hue, a sure sign his magical reserves were running dangerously low. This wasn't just stress; it was existential dread manifesting as a dermatological issue.

"Yes, Kevin," Azrael mumbled, his voice a low growl. "The 'really good wish'. Let's hear it." He braced himself for the inevitable – something involving a pet unicorn, a lifetime supply of pizza rolls, or, worst of all, world peace (the logistics alone were enough to induce a full-blown magical meltdown).

Kevin beamed, his eyes wide with an unnerving intensity. "I wish...for a cup of tea!"

Azrael blinked. A cup of tea? This was...unexpected. Almost disappointingly mundane after the previous day's events. He could handle a cup of tea. He *should* be able to handle a cup of tea. This was, after all, the simplest of wishes, a minor magical feat even for a genie whose powers had been somewhat diminished by years of dealing with inept humans.

He raised his hand, prepared to conjure a steaming mug of Earl Grey. The usual shimmering aura of magical energy, however, was notably...lackluster. Instead of the vibrant blue, it pulsed with a sickly yellow glow, much like a dying fluorescent lightbulb.

Then, things went wrong. Spectacularly wrong.

The floor beneath Kevin's feet began to tremble. A low rumble, like a disgruntled badger trapped in a washing machine, emanated from beneath the kitchen tiles. The air filled with the acrid smell of sulfur. Kevin yelped, his unicorn shirt momentarily forgotten in his panicked scramble for safety.

Azrael stared, aghast, as a miniature volcano erupted from the linoleum, spewing molten rock and scalding tea directly onto Kevin's newly acquired, and now ruined, pair of mismatched socks. A geyser of boiling water, infused with an odd amount of cinnamon, shot up into the air, narrowly missing the ceiling. Kevin, surprisingly, seemed more annoyed by the ruined socks than the near-volcanic eruption in his kitchen.

"My socks!" he wailed, his voice drowned out momentarily by the sound of miniature rocks clattering against the kitchen cabinets. "They were vintage!"

Azrael, meanwhile, felt a wave of exhaustion wash over him. He stumbled backward, his iridescent skin now a mottled green and yellow. His magic, apparently, had decided that a simple cup of tea was too demanding a task. Instead, it had interpreted the wish with its usual spectacular incompetence, creating a bizarre geyser of caffeinated magma. He could almost hear his magic whispering, "Too much pressure, too much stress! Give me a break!"

"I...I apologize," Azrael stammered, his voice barely a whisper. He felt a surge of self-pity, a genuine and intense pity for himself. He was a genie, supposed to grant wishes, and he couldn't even manage a simple cup of chamomile without starting a kitchen-based apocalypse.

He attempted another wave of magic, hoping to conjure a cleanup crew. Instead, a flock of miniature, slightly singed pigeons materialized, pecking at the remaining molten rock with an alarming degree of enthusiasm.

The rest of the afternoon continued in a similar vein of utter magical chaos. An attempt to repair the damage resulted in the kitchen transforming into a surreal landscape of swirling colours and misplaced furniture. Azrael tried to teleport the pigeons away, only to send them into a nearby hamster cage (the hamsters, strangely, seemed to enjoy the company). His attempts to conjure a replacement pair of socks for Kevin (vintage or otherwise) resulted in a small herd of alpacas appearing in the middle of the living room.

Each magical mishap seemed to drain Azrael's already depleted energy. He felt like a deflated balloon, slowly losing air. The slightest attempt at magic caused a minor, and sometimes major, catastrophe. He wanted to scream, to disappear, to retire to a quiet, magic-free existence in a dimension populated solely by sentient cacti who understood the importance of a low-key lifestyle.

As the sun set, casting long shadows across Kevin's chaotic kitchen, Azrael finally managed to conjure a single, lukewarm cup of tea –albeit one with a disturbingly high concentration of volcanic ash. He handed it to Kevin, who, remarkably, seemed satisfied.

"Thanks," Kevin mumbled, taking a sip. "Not bad, actually. Bit gritty, though."

Azrael just stared at him, wondering how he managed to remain so positive amidst a kitchen that resembled the aftermath of a small-scale geological disaster. Perhaps, Azrael thought, humanity's capacity for obliviousness was the true, untapped source of magic after all. At least his retirement plan seemed a little more solid now.

And maybe, just maybe, he'd invest in a better alarm clock. The plastic flamingo was proving to be a far greater magical threat than the teenagers he usually had to deal with. The idea of replacing it with a fluffy kitten instead was surprisingly calming.

Escape from the Teacup

The magician, a portly fellow named Cuthbert with a penchant for velvet robes and an alarming lack of common sense, hummed a tune that sounded suspiciously like a strangled cat fighting a vacuum cleaner. He waved his wand – a rather flimsy-looking thing made of what appeared to be polished driftwood – with the air of a man conducting a symphony of impending doom. Or perhaps a particularly inept game of charades. Azrael, having been inexplicably summoned from his (relatively) peaceful slumber within a chipped plastic flamingo, watched with a growing sense of dread.

Cuthbert's incantation, a jumble of words that sounded vaguely like a shopping list recited backwards, culminated in a puff of purple smoke that smelled suspiciously of burnt toast and regret. Instead of the majestic, fire-breathing dragon Cuthbert clearly intended to summon (judging by the rather impressive drawing on his rather less impressive spellbook), Azrael materialized – or rather, *dematerialized* – into the very bottom of a vintage teacup.

The teacup, a delicate porcelain thing adorned with whimsical cherubs who seemed to be mocking his predicament, was surprisingly comfortable. For a teacup. But it was a far cry from the spacious, if somewhat dusty, confines of the flamingo. Azrael tried to shout, to scream, to even stage a tiny, genie-sized tantrum, but his voice was muffled, his magical abilities inexplicably limited by the confines of his porcelain prison. He could feel the faint tremor of Cuthbert's panicked breathing above him.

"Oh, bother!" Cuthbert exclaimed, his voice a strangled squeak. He peered into the teacup, his face inches from Azrael's. Azrael attempted a regal wave, his arm barely visible above the rim. Cuthbert flinched. "I... I seem to have summoned something rather... small."

Azrael tried again, this time channeling all of his remaining magical energy into a telepathic blast: "GET ME OUT OF THIS THING!"

Cuthbert blinked, scratching his chin thoughtfully. "Did the teacup just... talk?" he muttered to himself, before concluding, "Nonsense. It's Tuesday. I must be hallucinating due to a lack of proper nourishment. Perhaps a crumpet?"

Azrael's internal monologue consisted of a series of increasingly colorful curses that would make a sailor blush. He tried a different approach. He concentrated, summoning a tiny, shimmering ball of magical energy, intending it to lift the teacup. Instead, the energy manifested as a miniature, sparkly lightning bolt that fried the stray hair on Cuthbert's wrist.

Cuthbert yelped, dropping the teacup with a delicate *clink*. Azrael bounced, narrowly avoiding a crack. This was getting ridiculous. He needed a bigger, better plan. Or at least, a less restrictive prison.

He tried whispering increasingly frustrated requests, shifting from polite pleas to outright demands. He even resorted to a dramatic, silent movie-style rendition of his plight, complete with exaggerated gestures and a highly expressive eyebrow. Cuthbert, bless his clueless heart, simply misinterpreted the whole thing as a very elaborate tea party for tiny porcelain fairies.

"Ah, yes," he said, stroking his chin once more. "The miniature woodland creatures seem rather displeased. Perhaps they'd like some honey?" He reached for a honey pot, completely ignoring the frantic vibrations emanating from the teacup.

Azrael realized he needed a more drastic measure. He focused his energies, channeling every ounce of his dwindling magic into one last, desperate attempt. He imagined himself soaring out of the teacup, a majestic, albeit miniature, genie returning to his rightful place in the world. Instead, he conjured a single, perfectly formed, miniature sugar cube that floated out of the cup and landed gently on Cuthbert's nose.

Cuthbert sneezed, a violent, honey-coated explosion that sent the teacup flying across the room. It landed, with a satisfying shatter, amidst a pile of spellbooks and a half-eaten crumpet.

Azrael, miraculously unharmed, found himself sprawled amongst the remnants of Cuthbert's magical misadventures. He surveyed the scene, a mixture of exhaustion and grudging triumph in his eyes. He was free. But his day was far from over. He sighed, the sound barely audible above the faint tinkling of broken porcelain. He knew that finding a new temporary abode, preferably one devoid of clueless magicians and surprisingly sentient teacups, was his next, and probably quite considerable, challenge.

His gaze fell upon a particularly dusty tome titled "Advanced Conjuring Techniques for the Ambitious (But Slightly Inept) Sorcerer." A wicked gleam appeared in his eye. Perhaps he could use this to his advantage, maybe even learn to summon a slightly less incompetent magician next time. Or at the very least, a self-cleaning flamingo.

The escape from the teacup, while undeniably exhilarating, had only served to further fuel his desire for a quiet, magical retirement. However, considering his current state, the task seemed further away than ever.

He could feel a nagging sense of responsibility. After all, he was still technically a genie, bound by some terribly archaic rules and even more terrible customer service standards. A long, weary sigh escaped his lips. He was a genie, condemned to serve humans, even the utterly, mind-bogglingly clueless ones.

This whole experience certainly added to the growing list of reasons why he was considering relocating to a dimension where the only magical beings were perfectly behaved, non-demanding, and preferably made of extremely soft, cloud-like substances.

His magical abilities, already somewhat depleted after the sugar cube incident, were slowly returning to normal. He took a moment to gather his thoughts, to plan his next move. He certainly wouldn't be trusting plastic flamingos anytime soon. He needed a new form of magical transportation, something more reliable, something... less likely to shatter into a thousand pieces. Perhaps a comfortable, oversized, self-cleaning slipper would be more appropriate for a genie of his particular disposition. It might even come with its own built-in retirement plan.

As he began to consider the merits of slipper-based transportation, he heard a faint whirring sound. He looked up to see a small, rather menacing-looking drone hovering in the air. It was equipped with a tiny, but unmistakably functional, net. Apparently, his escape from the teacup had merely been a brief respite from the inevitable chaos of the human world.

Azrael's eyes widened. This was far beyond the scope of any reasonably achievable retirement plan. He braced himself, muttering something under his breath that sounded suspiciously like "oh, for the love of..." before preparing for yet another unbelievably bizarre, entirely unexpected, and frustratingly comical adventure. He was going to need a very strong tea after this. And maybe a new career. Perhaps an accountant? They seemed to spend a lot of time hiding in their offices away from demanding clients. The thought, surprisingly, had a certain appeal.

Librarians Unintentional Release

Agnes Periwinkle, librarian extraordinaire (or at least, that's what her slightly chipped enamel name badge proclaimed), hummed a jaunty, if slightly off-key, tune as she navigated the labyrinthine shelves of the town library. Her spectacles perched precariously on her nose, threatening to topple at any moment, and a stray strand of grey hair escaped her bun, tickling her ear. Agnes, a woman whose organizational skills were inversely proportional to her memory, was attempting the impossible: alphabetizing the "Oversized and Misplaced" section. This was a task of Herculean proportions, a Sisyphean struggle against the tide of misplaced tomes and forgotten artifacts.

Today's particular challenge involved a particularly hefty collection of Victorian-era novels, each bound in what Agnes suspected was genuine leather (though she wasn't entirely sure, given her limited expertise in such matters). She heaved one particularly weighty volume onto the shelf, causing a slight tremor that sent a cascade of dust motes dancing in the weak afternoon sunlight filtering through the grimy windowpanes. Amongst the swirling dust, nestled precariously on the shelf's edge, sat Cuthbert's discarded teacup.

Agnes peered at the teacup, its chipped porcelain glistening in the dust-filled light. "Now, where did *that* come from?" she murmured, picking it up with a delicate touch. It felt strangely warm to the touch, almost vibrantly so. She tilted it slightly, peering inside. Nothing. Just a faint, shimmering haze. Agnes, ever the pragmatist, decided to simply place it in the "Objects of Uncertain Origin" box, a receptacle that housed everything from a petrified sausage roll to a rather suspicious-looking seashell.

As she attempted to place the teacup in the box, a puff of emerald green smoke erupted, engulfing Agnes in a cloud of sparkly, slightly acrid-smelling magic. Books tumbled from the shelves like panicked squirrels, landing with a resounding thud upon the hallowed carpeted floor. Agnes, momentarily blinded by the sudden burst of colour, yelped in surprise. When the dust settled, a disgruntled-looking genie, approximately the height of a particularly robust garden gnome, stood glaring at her.

He was dressed in what appeared to be a slightly tattered version of a sultan's robe, which, given the circumstances, looked more like a discarded tablecloth. His expression resembled a particularly grumpy badger that had just discovered its honey pot had been raided by a particularly mischievous honey badger.

"Are you alright, love?" Agnes asked, adjusting her spectacles, completely unfazed by the sudden appearance of a miniature, fuming genie. Librarians, it seemed, were made of sterner stuff.

Azrael, the aforementioned genie, glared at her. "Alright? Alright?! I've been trapped in a teacup for the better part of an afternoon. My aura is slightly singed, my temper is frayed beyond repair, and I've developed a mild aversion to Earl Grey. 'Alright' doesn't even begin to cover it!"

Agnes blinked. "Oh, I'm dreadfully sorry. I didn't realize it was...inhabited." She gestured towards the scattered books. "I seem to have caused quite a bit of a mess."

"A bit?" Azrael sputtered, gesturing wildly with a hand that shimmered faintly with residual magic. "My dear woman, you have unleashed chaos upon this unsuspecting library! And it's all your fault! All because of your... your... haphazard shelving technique!"

Agnes, surprisingly, did not take offense. "Well, it is the 'Oversized and Misplaced' section, you see. It tends to be... dynamic." She sighed, then pointed to the now-empty space on the shelf. "And there's clearly a problem with the shelf design. It seems awfully low for a teacup, doesn't it?"

Azrael stared at her, dumbfounded. He had expected outrage, perhaps a scream, maybe even a faint prayer. He had certainly not expected this level of unflappable calm. He'd faced down sorcerers, outwitted demons, and even once negotiated a peace treaty between a coven of particularly opinionated squirrels. But a librarian who treated the accidental release of a genie with such nonchalant acceptance? This was entirely new territory.

"You... you're not even slightly terrified?" he finally managed to stammer.

Agnes chuckled, a warm, comforting sound amidst the literary wreckage. "Terrified? Darling, I've dealt with far worse. Remember old Mr. Fitzwilliam and his insistence on borrowing only books with the letter 'Q' in the title? That, my dear genie, was truly terrifying."

Azrael found himself speechless. This woman was a force of nature, a whirlwind of placid acceptance in the midst of utter pandemonium. He took a deep breath, trying to regain his composure. He needed a strategy. A plan. Perhaps, he thought, offering a small, almost imperceptible sigh of resignation, he could bribe her with a rare first edition. That might at least buy him some time to figure out how to get back to his (relatively) peaceful existence before some other well-meaning, yet terribly incompetent individual decided he made a lovely addition to their collection.

"Right then," he began, trying to adopt a more authoritative tone, "Perhaps we could discuss... compensation for the... inconvenience. And the rather significant disruption to my afternoon nap."

Agnes beamed. "Oh, I have biscuits. Would you care for a ginger snap? We could discuss your... compensation... over a cuppa." She started picking up the scattered books, humming that same jaunty, slightly off-key tune as she surveyed the damage. Azrael, for the first time that day, felt a flicker of something akin to hope. Maybe, just maybe, this wouldn't be his worst day ever. After all, there was a very real chance of receiving decent biscuits and avoiding a potentially embarrassing confrontation with Mr. Fitzwilliam over the lack of 'Q' books in his latest borrowings. A small victory, but in these circumstances, a victory nonetheless. The thought of a biscuit, however, did distract him from the rather large problem of finding a way back to his home dimension, and how to explain his current predicament to his rather impatient landlord, a rather irritable and fire-breathing dragon named Ignis.

The task of restoring the library to its former order proved surprisingly collaborative. Agnes, with her uncanny ability to locate misplaced items, seemed to know exactly where each book belonged. Azrael, despite his initial grumbling, found himself oddly enjoying the process. He possessed a surprisingly deft touch when it came to organizing bookshelves, a skill he'd never realised he had.

And Agnes's seemingly endless supply of tea and biscuits helped immensely in calming his frayed nerves and allowing for a more civilised discussion regarding his 'compensation'. Perhaps a career change wasn't entirely off the table after all. A librarian's assistant who occasionally conjured lost books? It had a certain... charm.

The afternoon wore on, the chaos slowly receding into order. As the last book found its place, Agnes, beaming, turned to Azrael. "There, all done! Although, I must say, it's rather unusual to have a genie help with the Dewey Decimal System. I'll have to add that to my annual report."

Azrael stared at her, completely speechless. He had been summoned from a teacup, caused chaos, and ended up reorganizing a library. He really did need a new career. Perhaps this wasn't so bad after all.

Maybe, just maybe, retirement wouldn't be necessary after all. As long as he didn't have to work with Mr. Fitzwilliam. That thought sent a shiver down his spine that was far more frightening than any accidental summoning.

As Agnes prepared yet another cup of tea, Azrael cast a thoughtful glance at the shelves, at the neatly arranged books, and at the woman who had managed to find some sort of order in his chaotic arrival. Maybe, just maybe, being a genie wasn't so bad after all. At least, not as bad as it had initially seemed. He still desired a strong tea though. And possibly, a new, less chaotic career path. Perhaps a consultant on unusually shelved objects of uncertain origin. He would put that down on his next 'to-do' list, right after finding a way to properly explain his current situation to Ignis. That would need more than tea and biscuits, he suspected. It would require a whole other level of creative explanation. He had always been a creative genie, even if he wasn't particularly powerful. And for the first time that day, Azrael felt a very small, almost imperceptible smile tug at the corners of his lips. He'd faced worse. Much worse.

And he'd survived, thanks to a rather remarkable librarian and a surprisingly large supply of ginger snaps.

Reality TV Mayhem

The ginger snap crumbs still clung to Azrael's beard – a beard, he might add, that was far too prominent for a genie of his, ahem, *refined* stature. He was contemplating the existential dread of being mistaken for a particularly hirsute garden gnome when the cacophony began. Bright lights, blindingly cheerful voices, and the insistent whirring of cameras assaulted his senses. He'd escaped the library relatively unscathed, only slightly singed around the edges from a near-miss with a rogue curling iron (Agnes, bless her heart, had been experimenting with a new hair-styling technique). But this...this was a different level of chaos.

He found himself surrounded by a crew that resembled a flock of brightly colored, overly-caffeinated sparrows. They were flitting about, issuing rapid-fire instructions, and generally behaving as if the world would end if a single microphone cable was out of place. One particularly enthusiastic individual, who introduced himself as Barry – and whose name tag read "Barry – Best. Gaffer. Ever!" –pointed a camera directly at Azrael.

"Perfect! Absolutely perfect!" Barry shrieked, his voice echoing strangely in the surprisingly cramped space. "He's... he's... wonderfully... rustic! Exactly what we need for the 'Culinary Chaos'segment!"

Azrael blinked. Culinary Chaos? What in the seven circles of existential ennui was going on?

It transpired that Azrael, thanks to his unexpectedly voluminous beard and generally dishevelled appearance (a direct result of his recent teacup confinement and subsequent library escapade), had been mistaken for a particularly hirsute extra in a reality TV cooking show. The show, titled "Culinary Chaos," was a spectacularly uninspired display of amateur chefs battling it out with wildly impractical recipes and even wilder temper tantrums.

The producers, apparently operating on a level of logic only comprehensible to themselves, had decided that Azrael's appearance would add a touch of "authentic, earthy charm" to the already chaotic proceedings.

Azrael, however, had no intention of adding any charm, earthy or otherwise. He yearned for a quiet corner, a good book, and perhaps a lifetime supply of Earl Grey. The prospect of participating in a cooking competition, let alone one that embraced chaos as a key ingredient, filled him with a level of existential dread that even his rather limited magical powers couldn't alleviate.

"I assure you," he began, attempting to maintain a tone of refined exasperation, "I am not a culinary enthusiast. Nor am I an extra. I am... well, I'm a genie."

Barry, seemingly deaf to reason (or possibly just to anything that didn't involve a camera), waved a dismissive hand. "Rustic! That's it! We'll call him... Barnaby! Barnaby the Beard! He's going to be a sensation!"

Before Azrael could protest (he'd learned protesting was largely futile), he was shoved onto a small, brightly lit stage. Two contestants, a flamboyant baker with a penchant for exploding soufflés and a competitive chef with a questionable hygiene record, stared at him with varying degrees of suspicion and disgust.

The baker, a woman with hair the color of a sunset and a personality to match, chirped, "Who's the hairy hobbit?"

The chef, a man whose apron seemed to be perpetually stained with something vaguely orange and unsettling, grumbled, "Is he part of the judging panel? Because if so, I'm quitting."

The host, a man whose smile was as strained as a rubber band stretched to its limit, boomed into the microphone, "And now, for a surprise ingredient! Meet Barnaby the Beard, our special guest...uh... participant!"

Azrael's attempts to explain his true identity, to use his (admittedly limited) magic to whisk himself away, were continuously thwarted by the obliviousness of the production crew and the overwhelming din of the audience. He was forced to watch in horrified fascination as the flamboyant baker attempted to incorporate him into her latest culinary masterpiece: a seven-tiered cake decorated with what looked suspiciously like live garden gnomes (though he did wonder if they were related to him).

The chaos escalated. The exploding soufflés took out a camera, and a rogue whisk nearly struck Azrael in the eye. The competitive chef, in a fit of rage, tossed a whole roasted chicken at the audience. A small child started weeping inconsolably, and a security guard fainted.

Amidst the pandemonium, Azrael found a sliver of grim satisfaction. He had, quite accidentally, managed to cause even more culinary chaos than the show itself. This, he thought, was a remarkable achievement. He decided that perhaps the chaos he was bringing wasn't entirely his fault.

He did try, however, to subtly enhance the exploding soufflés, so they exploded with a satisfying 'poof' sound rather than a frightening 'bang'. This subtle act of magical mischief was the only thing keeping him sane.

Finally, after what felt like an eternity of culinary carnage, the show ended. Azrael, covered in flour, cake batter, and a lingering scent of despair, was released back into the wild. Or rather, back into the bewildering world of reality TV. He found Barry, still beaming, attempting to interview him about his "rustic charm".

"So, Barnaby," Barry chirped, adjusting his camera, "tell us, what was it like being part of Culinary Chaos?"

Azrael, unable to contain his exasperation any longer, let out a frustrated sigh that could rival a small hurricane. "It was," he muttered, adjusting his beard, which seemed to have gained several new, slightly sticky strands, "an experience I would not wish upon my worst enemy." He paused, then added with a hint of dry wit, "And believe me, I've had some truly awful enemies."

As he vanished into the night, leaving Barry to contemplate the baffling interview, Azrael realized that even a grumpy genie needed a break. Perhaps a far, far away dimension did indeed sound appealing. Preferably one with no reality TV shows, no exploding soufflés, and an unlimited supply of properly brewed Earl Grey tea. The next time Agnes offered him tea, he vowed to politely refuse.

He needed time to recover. He needed therapy, possibly. And definitely a new beard.

The Gurus Arrival

The shimmering portal, a byproduct of a particularly inept summoning spell (courtesy of a magician who apparently believed glitter was a key magical component), spat out a man radiating an almost offensively cheerful aura. He wore a shimmering, turquoise tracksuit, a smile that could curdle milk, and a name tag that read, with alarming enthusiasm, "Bartholomew 'Positive Vibes' Butterfield." Bartholomew 'Positive Vibes' Butterfield, Azrael noted with a groan that vibrated deep in his already-irritated genie bones, was a self-help guru. And apparently, Azrael was his next project.

Azrael, still recovering from the reality TV debacle (which involved a surprisingly aggressive chihuahua and a disastrous attempt at souffle-making), eyed Bartholomew with the kind of suspicion usually reserved for particularly aggressive squirrels. "You've got to be kidding me," he muttered, his voice a low rumble that barely registered above the incessant chirping of a flock of unusually philosophical pigeons who'd materialized out of nowhere earlier that day (another delightful consequence of the day's events). He hadn't even had time to sort through the leftover magical fallout from the librarian incident.

Bartholomew, blissfully unaware of the swirling chaos that was Azrael's current emotional and magical state, bounced on the balls of his feet, radiating enough positive energy to power a small city. "My dear fellow!" he boomed, extending a hand that seemed oddly sticky. "I've been *expecting* you! The universe has aligned, the chakras are singing, and your true potential is about to be unleashed!"

Azrael glared. "My 'true potential' involves a long nap in a dimension devoid of self-help gurus, sentient pigeons with a penchant for Brie, and reality TV crews," he grumbled, subtly trying to evaporate Bartholomew with a barely-there flick of his wrist. Nothing. His magic was still on the fritz.

Bartholomew, oblivious to the attempted magical assassination, pressed on. "Nonsense! I've mastered the art of positive affirmation, and I'm confident I can unlock the boundless power within you! Just repeat after me: 'I am powerful! I am magical! I am...' " He trailed off, searching for the perfect adjective. "I am... *radiant!* "

Azrael, internally rolling his eyes so hard he felt a migraine forming, tried a different tactic. "Listen, buddy," he began, his voice laced with barely-contained fury, "I'm a genie, not a self-esteem project. I grant wishes, I don't need to be 'unlocked.'"

"But think of the possibilities!" Bartholomew exclaimed, completely ignoring Azrael's rather pointed statement. "Imagine the magnificent wishes you could grant! With the power of positive thinking, you could create a world of peace, harmony, and unlimited cheese!" He paused, as if struck by an epiphany. "Yes, unlimited cheese! That's the key!"

Azrael's head began to throb. He'd initially hoped the reality TV crew's incompetence would be the low point of his day. He was so, so wrong. "Cheese isn't going to solve my existential crisis," he muttered. "My crisis involves poorly written genie contracts, overly enthusiastic librarians, and now, you."

The self-help guru, however, was completely undeterred. He launched into a series of motivational speeches, punctuated by vigorous hand gestures that sent books flying off shelves and caused a nearby potted plant to spontaneously combust (a surprisingly small explosion, given Azrael's usually impressive pyrotechnic abilities).

"Visualize success!" Bartholomew bellowed, his voice echoing through the room. "Envision a world where your magical powers are boundless! A world where wishes manifest instantly, and...and... you can conjure an infinite supply of gourmet croissants!"

Azrael's attempts to interrupt were met with an even more intense barrage of positive affirmations. "You are a magnificent being! You are overflowing with potential! You are... a... a... magnificent, croissant-conjuring, wish-granting powerhouse!" The pigeons, who seemed to have developed a taste for the increasingly chaotic energy in the room, cooed in apparent agreement.

The affirmations, predictably, backfired spectacularly. Instead of unleashing Azrael's "true potential," they resulted in a series of increasingly bizarre and unwanted manifestations. First, it was a sudden downpour of miniature, brightly colored umbrellas. Then a swarm of incredibly fluffy kittens materialized, each demanding attention and copious amounts of tuna. And then, a small army of squirrels wearing tiny top hats began marching across the floor, each carrying a miniature sign that read, "More Nuts!"

Azrael, surrounded by chaos, realized he'd made a grave error in underestimating the power of the guru's relentless positivity. His magic, instead of being amplified, was acting like a glitching video game, responding to Bartholomew's pronouncements in the most chaotic and unexpected ways.

The pigeons, meanwhile, were holding a spirited debate on the philosophical implications of unlimited cheese, a topic that seemed to absorb all their attention amidst the general chaos. One particularly vocal pigeon, perched on a stack of self-help books, was arguing vehemently about the existential dread inherent in the mass production of dairy products.

Bartholomew, however, remained unfazed. He saw the chaos not as a failure, but as a testament to Azrael's burgeoning power. "See?" he exclaimed, beaming. "The universe is responding! Your energy is exploding! You're... you're... absolutely magnificent!"

Azrael, completely overwhelmed, tried to make a desperate escape, but the portal that had brought Bartholomew had vanished. He was trapped, surrounded by philosophical pigeons, a marching army of squirrels, fluffy kittens demanding tuna, and a self-help guru who was absolutely convinced he was witnessing a miracle.

As the day spiraled further into absurdity, Azrael found himself wrestling with the undeniable truth: dealing with a self-help guru who misunderstood everything might actually be worse than being trapped in a teacup. He'd have gladly accepted a lifetime of teacup captivity to avoid the ongoing existential cheese crisis and the increasingly demanding top-hatted squirrels. His only hope was that the next portal would lead somewhere...anywhere...but here. This was, beyond any reasonable doubt, the worst day of his exceptionally long and often chaotic life as a genie. And he had a very strong feeling that it was only going to get worse before it got better, if it ever did. The pigeons, he noted with a sigh, were now arguing about the merits of vegan cheese. His day truly had no bottom.

Failed Affirmations

Bartholomew "Positive Vibes" Butterfield, radiating enough forced cheerfulness to power a small city, clapped Azrael on the shoulder with the enthusiasm of a particularly boisterous Labrador. "Right then, my ethereal friend!" he boomed, his voice echoing unnervingly in the cramped broom cupboard where Azrael currently resided. "Let's unlock your inner genie-potential! We'll unleash the power within!"

Azrael, whose inner genie-potential mostly consisted of a nagging headache and a profound desire for chamomile tea, winced. "I think I'm quite content with my current, uh, potential," he mumbled, trying to subtly shift away from Butterfield's overly enthusiastic patting. The man smelled faintly of sandalwood and desperation.

"Nonsense!" Butterfield declared, pulling out a brightly coloured chart titled "Achieving Genie Greatness: A 12-Step Programme." "Step one: Affirmations! Repeat after me: 'I am a powerful genie! My wishes manifest flawlessly! I am a master of magical manifestation!'"

Azrael, already regretting his life choices, reluctantly repeated the affirmations. Instead of a surge of magical energy, he experienced a mild tingling in his toes – which he immediately attributed to the dampness of the broom cupboard. "You seem... unimpressed," Butterfield observed, his smile wavering slightly.

"Impressed is not the word I'd use," Azrael sighed. He attempted to conjure a small flame, a simple test of his abilities. Instead, a miniature, slightly damp sneeze erupted from his fingertips. Butterfield blinked.

"Interesting," he said, his smile returning with renewed vigour. "A unique manifestation! Perhaps we need to adjust our approach. Let's try some visualization! Imagine yourself, Azrael, a magnificent, all-powerful genie, granting wishes with effortless grace!"

Azrael closed his eyes, trying to conjure the image. It was

surprisingly difficult. His usual image involved him slumped on a cloud, complaining about paperwork. Instead of a majestic genie, he ended up picturing himself wearing a tiny top hat and tap-dancing –a bizarre side effect of the top-hatted squirrels' earlier performance.

When he opened his eyes, Butterfield was staring at him with wide, slightly terrified eyes. Azrael attempted to conjure a cup of tea. The result was a small, slightly moldy mushroom that smelled faintly of burnt toast. Butterfield was no longer smiling.

"Perhaps...positive affirmations aren't your forte," Butterfield suggested tentatively. "How about... negative visualization? Imagine all the things you *don't* want to happen, and then use the power of reverse psychology to achieve the opposite!"

Azrael, at this point, was ready to accept anything that might end this torture. He visualized all the negative things: more inept summonings, more reality TV crews, more arguing pigeons, more top-hatted squirrels. He imagined Bartholomew Butterfield developing an uncontrollable obsession with interpretive dance.

The results were, to put it mildly, catastrophic. The broom cupboard started vibrating violently. A flock of extremely aggressive pigeons materialized, all wearing tiny top hats and carrying miniature teacups filled with what looked suspiciously like mustard. The moldy mushroom grew alarmingly large, forming a giant, sentient fungus that started demanding existential poetry.

Butterfield, his cheerful facade utterly shattered, let out a high-pitched shriek. "This is not what I intended!" he wailed, clutching his turquoise tracksuit. The tracksuit, responding to Azrael's involuntary negativity, spontaneously combusted into a small but fiery explosion, releasing a plume of faintly sandalwood-scented smoke.

Azrael, amid the chaos of poetry-spouting fungi, mustard-loving pigeons, and the lingering smell of burnt sandalwood, found himself strangely calm. He had reached peak absurdity. He might as well give up.

Butterfield, covered in soot and looking thoroughly traumatized, mumbled something about the power of manifestation being a "two-way street" and the need for "more rigorous self-assessment." He backed out of the broom cupboard, leaving Azrael surrounded by the remnants of his disastrous attempt at positive thinking.

Azrael sighed. He conjured a small, perfect cup of chamomile tea –a testament to his abilities when not hampered by positive vibes, reverse psychology, or top-hatted squirrels. He took a sip, savouring the quiet calm amidst the ongoing chaos. Retirement, he concluded, was still looking pretty good.

Butterfield's attempts to utilize alternative self-help techniques proved equally disastrous. He tried chanting, which resulted in a spontaneous monsoon of glitter and slightly off-key Gregorian chants. He attempted guided meditation, which triggered an infestation of philosophical garden gnomes who argued about the meaning of existence in rhyming couplets. He even resorted to aromatherapy, using essential oils which, instead of relaxation, manifested a swarm of bees with an unusual fondness for
interpretive dance and a talent for forming human-sized sculptures out of pollen. Each attempt served only to deepen Azrael's misery and highlight the sheer absurdity of the situation.

Azrael, while increasingly frustrated, found himself strangely captivated by the utter incompetence of it all. It was like watching a particularly inept magician attempt a grand illusion, only instead of rabbits and doves, they were producing sentient garden gnomes and philosophically inclined squirrels.

The day continued its relentless descent into chaos. The reality TV crew, having somehow survived the explosion of Butterfield's tracksuit, decided to document Azrael's supposed "magical transformation" as a result of the guru's coaching. Azrael's attempts to subtly steer them towards sensible wishes (like a lifetime supply of chamomile tea) were met with enthusiastic misunderstanding. The end result was a reality TV segment showcasing a bewildered genie, increasingly irritated pigeons, a philosophical garden gnome debate, and a pollen-sculpting bee colony.

By sunset, Azrael was utterly exhausted, his magical reserves depleted, and his patience completely eroded. The pigeons were now discussing the merits of existentialist cheese, the garden gnomes were composing a sonnet about the futility of self-help gurus, and the bees had started constructing a giant sculpture of Bartholomew Butterfield wearing nothing but a top hat and tap shoes.

As darkness fell, a new portal shimmered into existence, promising either a new adventure or, hopefully, blessed relief. Azrael could only hope that whatever or whoever emerged would have a better understanding of the concept of "sensible wishes" and, more importantly, a profound lack of interest in self-improvement techniques. Because, let's face it, a genie's life was hard enough without self-help gurus. The least they could do was not add to the existential crisis of a perpetually exhausted genie. The thought of another self-help guru made him shiver; he'd rather be trapped in a teacup for eternity.

Accidental Manifestations

Bartholomew, oblivious to Azrael's rapidly dwindling patience (and magical reserves), launched into a series of increasingly bizarre positive affirmations. "You are a magnificent genie! You are brimming with potent magic! You are... a fluffy cloud of pure genie-ness!" He punctuated each declaration with a vigorous thumbs-up, his smile so wide it threatened to split his face.

Azrael, trapped in the broom cupboard and surrounded by cleaning supplies that smelled suspiciously of lemon and despair, could only groan internally. The affirmations, instead of boosting his magical abilities, seemed to be having the opposite effect. A faint shimmering emanated from him, not the vibrant, golden glow he associated with powerful genie-magic, but rather a weak, flickering light resembling a dying firefly.

Suddenly, the cupboard door rattled violently. A chorus of cooing and squawking erupted, followed by a flurry of feathers and frantic flapping. The cupboard door burst open, revealing a flock of pigeons, not your average garden variety pigeons, but pigeons of extraordinary size, with intelligent, beady eyes and an air of profound dissatisfaction.

"Cheese," one pigeon demanded, its voice surprisingly deep and resonant. "We require cheese of the finest cheddar variety, aged to perfection."

Another pigeon, perched precariously on Bartholomew's head, added, "And a philosophical discourse on the nature of existence. Specifically, the existential dread inherent in the repetitive nature of pecking for crumbs."

Bartholomew, momentarily speechless, stared at the pigeons with wide, uncomprehending eyes. Azrael, however, was beginning to understand. Bartholomew's relentlessly positive affirmations, combined with Azrael's weakened state, had manifested the pigeons' desires, albeit in a rather unexpected form. The pigeons, it seemed, weren't just any pigeons; they were the embodiment of

Bartholomew's subconscious desires for intellectual stimulation and a refined palate, projected onto the nearest available avian species.

"I... I didn't mean to summon philosophical pigeons," Bartholomew stammered, his forced cheerfulness wavering for the first time. "I was just trying to... you know... unleash your inner genie-potential."

"Your 'inner genie-potential' apparently includes a penchant for summoning cheese-obsessed, existentialist pigeons," Azrael grumbled, his voice barely a whisper. He was starting to suspect that retirement wasn't just a viable option, but an absolute necessity.

The pigeons, ignoring Bartholomew completely, began to circle Azrael, their beady eyes assessing him with clinical precision. "He doesn't seem to possess enough cheddar to satisfy our collective philosophical musings," one pigeon declared, its tone laced with disappointment. "Perhaps a different approach is required."

Azrael felt a shiver run down his spine. This was worse than the teacup incident, worse than the reality TV crew, worse even than the librarian who'd accidentally unleashed him while searching for "The Complete Works of Edgar Allan Poe" (a rather unfortunate summoning experience involving a surprisingly large raven and an extensive discussion on the macabre). He was surrounded by philosophical pigeons who demanded cheese, and a self-help guru who seemed genuinely perplexed by the unfolding chaos.

Bartholomew, meanwhile, had begun to sweat profusely. His meticulously crafted positive aura was crumbling under the weight of the situation. He attempted another affirmation, a rather desperate, "We are all connected! We are all... cheese-loving, philosophical pigeons!"

The pigeons, however, remained unconvinced. Their collective gaze shifted from Azrael to a half-eaten packet of crisps tucked into Bartholomew's pocket. "Those," one declared with a distinct air of authority, "are a suitable, albeit inadequate, substitute for cheddar."

The next hour was a blur of frantic attempts to appease the philosophical pigeons. Bartholomew, guided by Azrael's increasingly sarcastic instructions, offered the crisps, followed by a rambling lecture on the inherent beauty of existentialism (which, to Azrael's surprise, seemed to mildly satisfy the pigeons). The pigeons, however, weren't easily appeased, launching into a heated debate about the merits of Nietzsche versus Sartre, their arguments punctuated by the crunching of crisps and the occasional aggressive peck at Bartholomew's perfectly coiffed hair.

Azrael, in a desperate attempt to regain some control over the situation, attempted a more powerful affirmation, a desperate plea for normalcy. "I am a powerful genie! This is under control! This is... just a Tuesday!"

The result was unexpected. A sudden gust of wind swept through the broom cupboard, flinging cleaning supplies across the room.

And from the chaos, a single, perfectly formed cheese wedge materialized, landing squarely in the midst of the philosophical pigeons. They instantly fell silent, their beady eyes fixed on the cheese. It was a moment of unexpected peace.

"Well," Azrael muttered, a hint of bewildered relief in his voice. "That was... something."

Bartholomew, still recovering from the ordeal, stared at the cheese wedge with a mixture of awe and terror. He looked at Azrael, his carefully constructed smile slightly askew. "So," he began, tentatively, "about unleashing your inner genie potential..."

Azrael interrupted him with a weary sigh. "Let's just call it a day. And perhaps next time, we stick to less... existential affirmations."

The pigeons, meanwhile, had begun their philosophical debate anew, their arguments now centered on the optimal way to consume the cheese wedge. Azrael wondered if he'd made the right choice in accepting Bartholomew's offer, but given the alternatives–another encounter with a reality TV crew or a librarian with questionable book-handling skills – he decided it was, for the time being, acceptable. He could always retire to a different dimension tomorrow. Or maybe next week. Possibly after he'd had a lengthy, stress-free nap in a dimension far, far away from inept humans, philosophical pigeons, and self-help gurus who believed that positive affirmations could solve any problem, even one involving an increasingly exasperated genie.

The next few days were a testament to the unpredictable nature of accidental manifestations. Bartholomew's attempts to further "unleash Azrael's inner genie-potential" resulted in a series of increasingly bizarre incidents. A flock of singing squirrels demanding royalties for their impromptu concert (a surprisingly good one, though Azrael had to pay them in peanuts); a swarm of overly polite bees who insisted on delivering him a meticulously crafted honey pot with apologies for the slight delay in its delivery; and a sentient potted plant that insisted on discussing the merits of organic fertilizer. Azrael was starting to think that perhaps a less "positive" approach might be beneficial for both himself and the well-being of the general public.

Perhaps he could focus on negative affirmations. "You are a terrible genie! You are full of incompetence! You are utterly, hilariously useless!" Azrael smiled, a mischievous glint in his eyes. The idea had a certain appeal. He decided to give it a go, and cautiously began to experiment. The first manifestation was a swarm of rather grumpy gnomes complaining about the lack of decent miniature furniture in the nearby antique store. It was a small step, but in Azrael's mind, a significant improvement over philosophical pigeons. The road to retirement, he realized, was paved with accidental manifestations, both positive and negative. And he was going to take it, one chaotic event at a time.

The Gurus Misunderstanding

Bartholomew, radiating an aura of misplaced self-confidence, mistook Azrael's increasingly frantic attempts to subtly end their session for enthusiastic participation. Azrael, attempting to subtly signal his desire for a swift exit (which involved a series of increasingly exaggerated yawns, the subtle shifting of his weight, and the silent invocation of every deity he could vaguely recall), was met with an escalating barrage of positive affirmations.

"You are releasing your inner genie power!" Bartholomew declared, his voice booming across the room. He gesticulated wildly, nearly knocking over a stack of self-help books with titles like *Unlock Your Inner Llama* and *Manifest Your Million-Dollar Yacht (Even if You're Currently Stuck on a Bicycle)* . "Feel the energy! Embrace the... the...genie-ness!"

Azrael let out a sigh that could have deflated a blimp.

Bartholomew, however, interpreted this as a triumphant exhale of pure genie magic.

"Yes!" he cried, clapping his hands together. "The breakthrough! I knew it! My techniques are unparalleled!" He grabbed Azrael's surprisingly soft arm (the teacup incident had left him rather damp, and therefore slightly less rigid than usual). "You are unlocking your potential! You're ready for the next level! Imagine the possibilities!"

Azrael imagined a quiet, solitary existence in a remote desert oasis, far from self-help gurus, reality TV crews, and the seemingly endless supply of inept magicians who kept summoning him from his otherwise peaceful, albeit slightly dusty, bottle. The oasis, he mused, would have excellent date palms and an uninterrupted supply of decent chamomile tea.

"Now," Bartholomew continued, oblivious to Azrael's internal escape plan, "we shall move on to the visualization exercise. Imagine yourself... radiating pure genie energy! A shimmering, iridescent cloud of... genie-ness!"

Azrael attempted a subtle throat-clearing maneuver, which Bartholomew interpreted as an enthusiastic affirmative grunt. He closed his eyes and began to hum a self-help mantra that sounded suspiciously like a badly-sung sea shanty.

Azrael tried a different tactic. He subtly transformed a nearby potted plant into a small, very grumpy cactus. Bartholomew, however, was too engrossed in his inner genie journey to notice the sudden spike in the room's irritability levels.

"Feel the power flowing through you," Bartholomew chanted, his voice now a rhythmic drone that threatened to induce an involuntary nap in Azrael, a far more appealing prospect than whatever self-help nonsense was about to unfold. "Feel the... the...genie-ness!" He punctuated each word with a vigorous head bob that would have made a bobblehead doll jealous.

Azrael, fueled by desperation and a dwindling supply of magical energy, decided to try a more direct approach. He attempted to teleport himself to his aforementioned oasis, a shimmering image of date palms momentarily flickering in his mind. But the teleportation spell fizzled, resulting in a minor tremor and a sudden flurry of glitter that covered Bartholomew in a fine layer of sparkling dust.

"Oh my goodness!" Bartholomew exclaimed, beaming. "The glitter! It's a sign! A sign of... magnificent genie-ness!" He began to enthusiastically rub the glitter into his face, muttering about positive affirmations and the cosmic alignment of his inner genie self.

Azrael, defeated but not entirely broken, resolved to try a different strategy. He decided on a slow, drawn-out, dramatic collapse. He slumped against the nearest armchair with a sigh that shook the very foundations of the room.

Bartholomew, mistaking this for an impressive display of post-visualization exhaustion, beamed approvingly. "You did it!" he exclaimed. "You've reached peak genie-ness! Now, let's discuss your next breakthrough: Mastering the Art of Manifestation Through Positive Thinking in a Multi-Dimensional Genie Reality!"

Azrael groaned inwardly. His retirement plans were clearly going to require more than just a simple teleportation spell. Perhaps he could manifest a giant, inescapable pillow. Or a portal to the nearest interdimensional Starbucks. Or maybe, just maybe, a lifetime supply of chamomile tea – and perhaps some serious earplugs.

His next attempt at escape involved a strategically placed sneeze, which he managed to make sound like a small, contained explosion. Bartholomew, predictably, took this as a sign of burgeoning genie power, enthusiastically declaring, "You're releasing pent-up genie energy! I knew it! My methods are infallible!" He then proceeded to demonstrate a series of increasingly complex breathing exercises, which involved a significant amount of huffing and puffing, and the occasional whoop of self-congratulation.

Azrael, at this point, was contemplating the use of more drastic measures. Maybe he could accidentally manifest a swarm of particularly aggressive honeybees? Or a sudden, inexplicable rainstorm indoors? Or perhaps a horde of philosophical squirrels.

The possibilities, as chaotic as they were, began to fill him with a renewed sense of mischievous glee. Retirement might be a long way off, but the journey was proving to be far more entertaining than he'd anticipated. The sheer absurdity of it all was, ironically, a small comfort in the midst of the chaos.

He'd long since given up on subtle cues. Bartholomew was clearly beyond redemption. This, Azrael realised with a wry smile, was a battle he couldn't win by playing nice. The war for his freedom was now officially underway. And it would be fought with the weapons he had at his disposal - accidental manifestations, exasperated sighs, and the ever-present threat of a poorly-executed teleportation spell. The final battle of wills began, each attempt to escape followed by Bartholomew's unwavering belief in Azrael's supposed progress.

Each misfired spell became a testament to the guru's misguided optimism, and each sigh of frustration fueled his unyielding enthusiasm. It seemed the only path to freedom was to lead

Bartholomew down the rabbit hole of his own self-deception.

And so, the battle raged on, a comedic duel between a grumpy genie and an utterly clueless self-help guru, a clash of wills set against a backdrop of accidentally summoned gnomes, philosophical squirrels, glitter, and an overwhelming sense of surreal absurdity. It was a day that Azrael would likely recount in his retirement, albeit with many embellishments, possibly including a fleet of miniature flying elephants. After all, exaggeration was, he mused, an art form in itself. And one he was about to perfect.

A Very Positive Outcome

Bartholomew, brimming with a self-satisfaction that could power a small city, finally declared the session concluded. He bounced on the balls of his feet, radiating an almost tangible aura of smugness.

"Magnificent!" he boomed, adjusting his ridiculously oversized turquoise turtleneck. "Absolutely magnificent! I feel...reborn! Ready to conquer the world! Or at least, write my next best-selling self-help book: *Unlocking Your Inner Genie* ."

Azrael, meanwhile, felt anything but reborn. He resembled a deflated soufflé, his usual shimmering turquoise now a dull, slightly greenish hue. The gnomes, initially summoned as a desperate attempt to create a distraction (they'd ended up embroidering tiny hats for the philosophical squirrels), were now harmoniously singing off-key renditions of Gregorian chants. The glitter, which had initially been a byproduct of a particularly disastrous spell gone awry, clung stubbornly to his already dishevelled beard.

"Reborn," Azrael muttered, his voice a low growl. "More like thoroughly, irrevocably, glitter-bombed." He tried to subtly conjure a whirlwind to whisk away the annoyingly persistent sparkles, but instead, he accidentally summoned a flock of miniature, inexplicably dapper penguins. They waddled around his feet, chirping cheerfully.

Bartholomew, completely oblivious to Azrael's simmering rage and the increasingly bizarre additions to their impromptu meditation session, continued his pronouncements. "This experience," he declared, "has confirmed everything I've ever believed! The power of positive thinking! The universe conspires to help those who dare to dream! And gnomes! Apparently, gnomes are excellent hat-makers!" He beamed, completely missing the subtle death glare Azrael was directing his way.

Azrael attempted a new tactic: sheer, overwhelming boredom. He yawned, a yawn of such epic proportions that it threatened to swallow the entire room. He stretched, cracking his nonexistent genie bones with a series of exaggerated pops and clicks. He even attempted a mime routine depicting a particularly dull episode of daytime television, complete with dramatically slow hand gestures and a vacant stare.

Nothing worked. Bartholomew remained utterly impervious to his subtle (and not-so-subtle) attempts at escape. He even mistook Azrael's attempts to silently summon a portal to another dimension as a form of advanced yogic breathing exercise.

"I can feel the energy flowing!" Bartholomew exclaimed, his voice echoing with unwavering conviction. "It's...whirlwindy! And penguin-y!" He giggled, completely charmed by the little tuxedoed creatures who were now attempting to steal a bite from Azrael's already-too-small teacup.

Azrael's frustration reached a new, previously unknown level of intensity. He considered summoning a horde of particularly grumpy badgers, but feared the potential collateral damage. He briefly toyed with the idea of turning Bartholomew into a potted fern, but decided against it. The paperwork involved in reversing such a drastic transformation was more than he could handle at that moment.

Then, a thought struck him, a spark of genuine, albeit grudging, admiration igniting in the depths of his genie despair.
Bartholomew, in his glorious, oblivious self-assuredness, had somehow achieved something extraordinary. He'd taken a chaotic, glitter-strewn, gnome-infested encounter with a deeply disgruntled genie and somehow spun it into a life-affirming, self-help epiphany.

It was, in its own absurd way, a masterpiece. A testament to the power of positive thinking, even if that positive thinking was utterly and completely misplaced. Azrael had to admit, a tiny part of him—a part buried deep under layers of magical exhaustion and glitter—felt a grudging respect for the man's unshakeable belief in himself.

As Bartholomew continued to gush about his transformative experience, detailing his plans to incorporate penguin-assisted meditation into his next workshop, Azrael found himself unexpectedly amused. He'd originally planned to spend the rest of his eternity far, far away from humans, but now, a strange thought entered his mind. Perhaps, just perhaps, there was a certain comedic value to these encounters, a perverse sort of entertainment to be gleaned from the utterly unpredictable chaos of human interaction.

The penguins, having finished their assault on Azrael's teacup, began to sing a surprisingly harmonious rendition of "Happy Birthday." Bartholomew, mistaking this as further proof of the universe's benevolent alignment, started to dance. Azrael, watching the absurd spectacle unfold, couldn't help but crack a rare, weary smile. Maybe retirement could wait. Perhaps there were still a few more chapters left to write in this unexpectedly hilarious saga of human folly and a genie's increasingly eccentric attempts to maintain a semblance of control.

He even considered, just for a fleeting moment, writing a chapter titled "The Unexpected Joys of Penguin-Assisted Meditation" for Bartholomew's next best-selling self-help manual. After all, the man seemed to need all the help he could get. And perhaps, just perhaps, Azrael's unique brand of chaotic assistance might be exactly what the world needed – if only it could handle it. The squirrels, now sporting tiny, perfectly embroidered hats, seemed to agree with a series of philosophical nods and chirps. Even the gnomes were nodding in agreement, their Gregorian chants morphing into a surprisingly catchy tune about the importance of glitter in one's personal growth. The chaotic energy of the room seemed to intensify, as if all the universe's weirdness was coalescing into one gloriously absurd moment.

Azrael sighed, a sound that somehow managed to be both weary and amused. This was definitely a day he'd be recounting for centuries to come, and perhaps, embellishing even more fantastically than he'd initially planned. After all, every good story needed a touch of magic – or at least, a whole lot of inexplicable glitter and surprisingly well-dressed penguins. He closed his eyes, briefly envisioning a future filled with more bizarre encounters, more self-help gurus with questionable wisdom, and perhaps, a surprisingly successful side hustle as a consultant for penguin-assisted yoga retreats. The possibilities, he had to admit, were remarkably absurd, and wonderfully enticing. The world, even with its chaotic and perpetually clueless humans, was strangely, undeniably, full of potential for a genie with a mildly grumpy disposition and less magical power than advertised. And as Bartholomew's laughter echoed through the room, accompanied by the surprisingly soulful singing of dapper penguins, Azrael knew, with a certainty that even the most powerful genie couldn't deny, that he was in for a ride.

He just hoped he'd remember to bring more teacups next time. And maybe, a vacuum cleaner. The glitter, he reflected, was going to be a serious problem. But honestly? He wouldn't have it any other way. The sheer, breathtaking absurdity of it all was, in its own peculiar way, utterly magical. And that was something even a slightly grumpy, underpowered genie couldn't deny. The universe, it seemed, had a peculiar sense of humor, and Azrael, against all odds, was starting to appreciate the joke. He might even learn to laugh along with it, one day. Maybe. But perhaps he'd start by finding a very effective glitter remover. That, at least, seemed a more urgent priority than contemplating his retirement. For now, at least.

The Magicians Apology

The magician, a portly man with a surprisingly flamboyant mustache that seemed to vibrate with nervous energy, waddled towards Azrael, who was currently perched precariously on the rim of a rather chipped teacup, feeling considerably less majestic than a genie ought to. The magician, whose name Azrael had gleaned from a hastily scrawled business card (it read, rather dramatically, "Bartholomew Butterscotch, Purveyor of Mystical Merriment"), cleared his throat, a sound like gravel gargling with cough syrup.

"Right then," Bartholomew began, adjusting his ridiculously oversized spectacles, "about that... incident with the teacup. Terribly sorry about that, old boy. Rather unfortunate, wouldn't you say?" He offered a small, apologetic wave, the gesture somehow managing to seem both insincere and profoundly irritating.

Azrael, whose magical powers were still somewhat hampered by his recent ordeal involving sentient pigeons, a reality TV crew, and a self-help guru who believed affirmations could cure anything (including Azrael's current predicament), let out a sigh that sounded suspiciously like the deflating of a punctured balloon. "Unfortunate? Bartholomew, my dear man, I was trapped inside a teacup! A *teacup* ! I, Azrael, genie of considerable (though currently diminished) power, was reduced to the size of a particularly plump gnat!" He emphasized the last part with a dramatic flourish, though the effect was somewhat muted considering his diminutive size.

Bartholomew blinked, clearly unimpressed. "Yes, well," he mumbled, fiddling with a rather ornate silver spoon, "accidents happen. Magic is a fickle mistress, you know. One minute you're conjuring delightful doves, the next you're... well, you were in a teacup." He shrugged, as if the whole thing was a minor inconvenience, akin to forgetting to water the petunias.

Azrael considered this for a moment, his tiny form trembling with barely contained rage. "Fickle mistress? This wasn't a matter of a misplaced spell, Bartholomew. This was a blatant disregard for the fundamental principles of safe magical practice! I could have been seriously injured! Or, worse, forced to participate in another reality television cooking competition!" The mere thought sent a shiver of horror through him.

Bartholomew looked thoroughly confused. "Cooking competition? Oh, you mean the one with the... um... very hairy extra?" he asked, the memory apparently registering as something mildly amusing. Azrael groaned inwardly.

Before Azrael could launch into a detailed explanation of the horrors of forced televised culinary combat, a high-pitched squeak pierced the air. A small, ginger cat, sporting a tiny bow tie, sauntered into view, its tail held high like a miniature royal standard. Following closely behind was the forgetful librarian, Miss Agatha Plumtree, a woman whose organizational skills were inversely proportional to her enthusiasm for afternoon tea.

"Oh my," Miss Plumtree exclaimed, her eyes widening as she spotted Azrael in the teacup. "Bartholomew, dear, you haven't been at your magic again, have you?" She spoke as if it were a perfectly normal occurrence for magicians to accidentally trap genies in teacups. Azrael was beginning to think it was.

This time, it wasn't just a tea party; it was a full-fledged, chaotic tea party. Miss Plumtree had brought out her finest china, a selection of biscuits that looked suspiciously like they'd been gnawed on by something small and furry (likely the ginger cat), and a rather impressive selection of jams. A squirrel, seemingly uninvited, had joined the gathering, diligently attempting to pilfer sugar cubes. The scene was ludicrous, a bizarre tableau of miniature mayhem.

Azrael, still trapped in the teacup, watched in stunned silence as Miss Plumtree poured tea into a delicate porcelain cup – a cup that was, incidentally, significantly larger than his current prison. The sheer injustice of it all was almost enough to break the last vestiges of his composure. He attempted to summon a small gust of wind to tip the teacup, a desperate gambit for freedom. But his magic, weakened by stress and the indignity of the situation, sputtered and died. All he managed was a tiny puff of air that ruffled the ginger cat's bow tie.

The squirrel, emboldened by the general lack of order, leaped onto the table, scattering sugar cubes in a frantic sugar-fueled escapade. The ginger cat, possibly spurred on by this act of brazen rebellion, decided to join the party, batting at the sugar cubes with a gleeful air of mischief.

Seeing his opportunity, Azrael focused his remaining energy. He wouldn't simply escape, he would engineer a spectacular, chaotic escape. Using a combination of strategically placed sugar cubes, a well-aimed sneeze from the ginger cat (a sneeze that sent a shower of sugar cubes flying), and a poorly timed jump from the squirrel, he managed to create a miniature avalanche of sugary chaos. In the resulting confusion, the teacup wobbled, teetered, and finally, with a resounding clatter, fell to the floor, shattering into a thousand tiny pieces.

Azrael, freed at last, lay amidst the debris of his porcelain prison, covered in sugar and feeling remarkably less grumpy than one might expect. He looked up to see Bartholomew staring at the wreckage with a mixture of horror and bewilderment. Miss Plumtree was busy scooping up the escaped sugar cubes, while the squirrel and ginger cat were engaged in a surprisingly amicable sharing of sugar-coated biscuits.

He took a deep breath, the scent of sugar and impending chaos filling his nostrils. He had endured inept magicians, reality TV, and philosophical pigeons. He'd been trapped in not one, but two teacups. And yet, somehow, he felt an odd sense of accomplishment. Maybe retirement could wait. There was still so much chaos to be encountered, so many absurd situations to be navigated. He just hoped the next adventure wouldn't involve another tea party. Especially one with a particularly aggressive squirrel. Or a ginger cat with a penchant for sugar-induced sneezes.

He sighed, already feeling the familiar creeping tendrils of exasperation. This was, after all, only the beginning of what promised to be another hilariously awful day.

A Second Teacup Trap

Bartholomew Butterscotch, Purveyor of Mystical Merriment (as his card so proudly proclaimed), blinked, his mustache twitching like a startled caterpillar. He'd meant to free Azrael, the grumpy genie currently residing in a chipped teacup, but his incantation, apparently, had a rather...flexible interpretation of "release."Instead of freeing Azrael, he'd somehow managed to shrink the teacup, Azrael included, to about the size of a thimble. Azrael, now a miniature, disgruntled genie, glared up at Bartholomew from his porcelain prison.

"Are you seriously telling me," Azrael squeaked, his voice a high-pitched whine that was surprisingly effective, "that you, a self-proclaimed 'Purveyor of Mystical Merriment,' have just shrunk me further? And into an even *more* precarious teacup?"

Bartholomew, his face a mask of horrified apology, stammered, "I...I... I aimed for 'liberation'! A shimmering, majestic liberation! Not...miniaturization!" He frantically fumbled through a bag overflowing with oddly shaped crystals, dried herbs, and what appeared to be a half-eaten gingerbread man. "There must be something here... a counter-spell... a... a... shrinking-reversal-potion?"

Azrael, clinging to the rim of the tiny teacup with surprising agility, sighed dramatically. "Potion? Bartholomew, my dear, your bag looks like it was raided by a goblin with a particularly sweet tooth and a questionable sense of hygiene. I wouldn't trust anything in there to cure a common cold, let alone undo your miniature magical mishap."

Bartholomew, undeterred by the genie's pessimism, pulled out a vial filled with a viscous, iridescent liquid that shimmered with an unsettling purple glow. "This is it! My grandmother's... uh... size-restoration elixir! Guaranteed to... well, it's supposed to restore things to their original size. Mostly." He uncorked the vial and, with trembling hands, dribbled a single drop onto the tiny teacup.

Instead of returning to its normal size, the teacup began to glow with a feverish intensity. It pulsed, it shimmered, it hummed with an energy that could only be described as "uncomfortably enthusiastic." Then, with a satisfying *pop* , it vanished entirely.

Azrael, for a heart-stopping moment, felt nothing. Then, a peculiar sensation of weightlessness, followed by a sudden, rather unpleasant thud. He found himself lying on a plush, velvety surface–the inside of Bartholomew's rather impressive mustache.

"Well, that's... unexpected," Azrael muttered, brushing a stray hair from his face. "Though, I must admit, the mustache has a surprisingly soft landing."

Bartholomew, meanwhile, was frantically searching his bag again, his mustache vibrating with a panicked energy that threatened to tickle Azrael into unconsciousness. "Oh dear, oh dear, oh dear! I seem to have... misplaced the counter-counter-spell! The one that reverses the accidental... uh... mustache-transportation spell!"

Azrael groaned. "Mustache-transportation spell? Is that even a real thing, Bartholomew?"

"It is now," Bartholomew declared with a dramatic flourish, completely ignoring Azrael's question. "I'm quite the innovator, you know. Always pushing the boundaries of mystical merriment."

Azrael, resigned to his fate, decided to make the best of a bad situation. He looked around, taking in the surprisingly comfortable surroundings. Bartholomew's mustache, he discovered, was remarkably warm and surprisingly absorbent. It was like resting in a cloud of slightly sweaty, sugary goodness.

"Well," he said, settling deeper into the mustache, "at least it's not another teacup."

The next hour proved to be a surprisingly relaxing experience for Azrael. He found the gentle vibrations of Bartholomew's mustache quite soothing, almost meditative. He'd closed his eyes and almost drifted off when a high-pitched sneeze erupted from somewhere deep within the mustache's cavernous depths. Azrael was showered in a fine mist of sugar and... something else. Something vaguely floral and decidedly less pleasant.

"Apologies!" Bartholomew mumbled from somewhere above. "It seems my recent consumption of excessively sugary gingerbread has aggravated a pre-existing condition. A particularly pungent sneezing affliction, you see."

Azrael coughed, wiping his face with a miniature handkerchief (he always kept a spare). "I think I'd rather be in a teacup."

The sneeze-induced chaos continued for another ten minutes, a series of increasingly violent eruptions that sent Azrael tumbling through the thick, velvety undergrowth of Bartholomew's mustache.

It was exhilarating in its own chaotic way. At one point, Azrael even encountered what he believed to be a lost colony of dust bunnies, happily residing in the lusher parts of Bartholomew's facial landscaping. They were surprisingly philosophical, discussing the existential dread of being a perpetually overlooked piece of fluff.

Finally, after what felt like an eternity, the sneezing stopped.

Bartholomew, looking pale and somewhat depleted, began the painstaking process of extracting Azrael from his hirsute prison. He employed a series of tweezers, small brushes, and a surprisingly effective vacuum cleaner attachment (miniature, of course, suitable for delicate mustache maintenance).

The extraction process was as bizarre as one might expect. Azrael, feeling slightly disoriented and smelling strongly of sugar, ginger, and something vaguely floral, was finally freed. He landed, somewhat unceremoniously, on a pile of Bartholomew's spellcasting paraphernalia. He brushed himself off, feeling rather like a well-loved, albeit slightly disheveled, stuffed toy.

"Right then," Azrael said, regaining his composure. "I believe that concludes my unfortunate encounter with your 'mystical merriment'. I trust there won't be a third teacup incident?"

Bartholomew, still recovering from his sneezing fit, nodded vigorously. "Absolutely not! I shall confine myself to less...

unpredictable magic from now on. Perhaps some simple card tricks? Or perhaps... interpretive dance?"

Azrael considered this. "Interpretive dance? You're certain that wouldn't result in a fourth teacup incident?"

Bartholomew, wisely, remained silent. He had learned his lesson, or at least, he hoped he had. Azrael, however, wasn't so sure. After all, this was Bartholomew Butterscotch, Purveyor of Mystical Merriment – and that, Azrael knew, was a recipe for disaster. A deliciously, chaotically disastrous recipe. He sighed. Retirement was sounding more and more appealing by the minute. Perhaps a nice, quiet dimension, far away from inept magicians and their overly ambitious spells... Perhaps. But only perhaps. The allure of chaos, of absurd human encounters, was a powerful siren song indeed. He wasn't ready to give up on it just yet. Not quite. There was still so much wonderfully awful potential waiting to be unleashed. And who knew what further mishaps awaited him? It was, after all, just another day in the life of a perpetually inconvenienced genie.

An Unexpected Tea Party

Agnes Periwinkle, librarian extraordinaire (and possessor of a rather alarming collection of novelty teacups), discovered the miniature teacup – and its disgruntled inhabitant – nestled amongst a pile of overdue library books on Arthurian legends. She'd been hunting for a particularly elusive copy of "Sir Gawain and the Green Knight"(the one with the sparkly cover, naturally), when she spotted the tiny, chipped porcelain.

"Well, isn't that just the cutest thing?" Agnes cooed, her spectacles perched precariously on her nose. She picked up the teacup, completely oblivious to the miniature, furious genie currently inhabiting its depths. Azrael, for his part, was attempting to fashion a tiny escape ladder out of a stray bookworm, with minimal success. The worm, it seemed, had other plans for its life. Mainly, eating.

Agnes, humming a jaunty tune, decided the miniature teacup would be the perfect centerpiece for her afternoon tea party. A tea party, she reasoned, was exactly what was needed to alleviate the stress of dealing with overdue books and the general chaos inherent in managing a library frequented by cats, squirrels, and the occasional rogue badger.

And so, the unexpected tea party commenced. Agnes, in her sensible cardigan and sensible shoes, laid out a miniature feast fit for a thimble-sized king. There were itty-bitty cucumber sandwiches, painstakingly crafted from bread crumbs and a particularly cooperative radish; miniature scones, the size of pebbles, dotted with dollops of jam made from a single, exceptionally generous strawberry; and, of course, tea. Plenty of tea. Served in thimbles, naturally.

The guests arrived in a flurry of fur and fluff. Mittens, a ginger tabby with a penchant for napping in the stacks; Jasper, a sleek black cat with a perpetually unimpressed expression; and Pip, a squirrel whose understanding of social etiquette was, shall we say, limited. Pip primarily attended the tea party because he smelled the aforementioned exceptionally generous strawberry.

Azrael, observing this miniature social gathering from within the teacup, felt a surge of... something. It wasn't exactly amusement, but it wasn't exactly utter despair either. The cats, engrossed in their own feline drama involving a particularly enticing dust bunny, paid him little attention. Pip, on the other hand, was displaying an unnerving interest in the miniature sandwiches, his tiny paws surprisingly deft at maneuvering the breadcrumb-radish concoctions.

Agnes, oblivious to the genie's presence, continued to pour tea, her voice a cheerful counterpoint to the rustling of leaves and the occasional meow. She made small talk with the cats (mostly consisting of soothing murmurs and gentle head scratches) and attempted to engage Pip in conversation. This resulted in Pip chattering excitedly in squeaky squirrel language, which Agnes interpreted as enthusiastic agreement about the quality of the strawberry jam.

Azrael, meanwhile, found himself oddly captivated. He'd expected chaos and pandemonium, perhaps a full-scale battle between the cats and the squirrel, involving strategically placed miniature teacups as weapons. Instead, he found a surprising serenity. The miniature world was a world of quiet moments – the gentle clinking of thimbles, the soft purring of cats, the frantic munching of a squirrel, a serene librarian humming a cheerful tune – a complete contrast to the usually hectic world of human interaction he was accustomed to.

The absurdity of it all began to seep in, a slow, insidious chuckle working its way up from his miniature chest. Here he was, a genie of supposed power, trapped in a teacup, watching a tea party for cats, a squirrel, and a completely oblivious librarian. The irony was palpable, rich, and almost... enjoyable.

Suddenly, Pip, in a moment of exuberant squirrel energy, knocked over a thimble of tea. The tiny spill splashed onto the edge of the teacup, creating a tiny ripple effect that momentarily jostled Azrael. He let out a tiny, involuntary sneeze, a sound barely audible above the purring of Mittens.

Agnes, hearing the faintest of sounds, peered into the teacup. Her eyes widened. "Goodness gracious!" she exclaimed, "It's a tiny genie!"

The cats, startled by her outburst, momentarily stopped their dust bunny battle. Pip froze, a half-eaten breadcrumb still clenched in his tiny paw.

Azrael, caught red-handed (or, rather, red-tea-stained), sighed dramatically. "Yes," he admitted, "it's me. And quite frankly, I'm starting to rather enjoy this absurd tea party." He paused, glancing at the miniature sandwiches. "Though I must admit," he added, "the cucumber sandwiches could use a little more seasoning."

Agnes, far from being horrified, seemed delighted. "Oh, marvelous!" she declared. "A genie at my tea party! This is even better than the time I accidentally summoned a flock of particularly talkative pigeons!" She produced a tiny, silver fork from her pocket. "Do try the scones. They're my own recipe."

And so, the miniature tea party continued, now with the unexpected addition of a grumpy but surprisingly adaptable genie.

The cats remained indifferent, Pip devoured the remaining miniature scones with gusto, and Agnes regaled Azrael with stories of rogue badgers and mysteriously disappearing books. Azrael, in turn, shared some of his own (somewhat embellished) stories about his magical adventures, and the very real frustration of dealing with incompetent humans. It wasn't retirement exactly, but it was remarkably close to the quiet peace he'd craved, minus the badgers. The tea, however, remained outstanding.

Later, as Agnes tidied up the miniature remnants of the tea party, she carefully placed the teacup containing Azrael onto a shelf filled with books on comparative mythology. Azrael, feeling strangely content, decided to embrace the absurdity of his current situation. Maybe retirement wasn't necessary after all. After all, he could have far worse problems than a slightly overzealous librarian and an insatiable squirrel. And, he thought with a tiny genie smile, the tea had been absolutely delightful. Perhaps he could get the recipe.

The next few days saw Azrael participating in more unexpectedly delightful miniature events: miniature croquet matches with the cats (Jasper cheated relentlessly), miniature treasure hunts organized by Pip (the treasure was invariably a discarded acorn), and miniature story-telling sessions hosted by Agnes, during which Azrael regaled her with tales of his life as a genie, greatly embellished for dramatic effect.

The miniature world, surprisingly, was full of charm and unexpected camaraderie. Azrael found himself adjusting to the change in perspective, and realized that maybe, just maybe, the human world, when viewed from a slightly lower vantage point, held a distinct charm that had been overlooked in his usual, full-sized experiences. It wasn't just about avoiding disasters; it was about the quiet moments of absurdity that made life interesting.

One evening, while listening to Agnes reading aloud from a book of fairy tales, a thought struck Azrael. Maybe, just maybe, he didn't need to escape the human world after all. Perhaps, there was a kind of magic in the chaos, in the unexpected twists and turns, in the surprisingly delightful company of cats, squirrels, and overly enthusiastic librarians. It was a far cry from the majestic, powerful genie existence he once imagined, but somehow, it felt... right.

Right enough to consider extending his stay, at least until Agnes finished that very intriguing book on the history of teacups. After all, he had a feeling there were many more unexpected tea parties to be had, and he wouldn't have it any other way. The tea, after all, was excellent.

Escape from the Tea Party

The tea party, it turned out, was even more chaotic than Agnes's usually well-organized library. It wasn't the usual polite sipping and polite conversation. Oh no, this was a whirlwind of sugar-fueled children, a runaway chihuahua named Princess Fluffybutt III (apparently, the lineage was important), and a surprisingly competitive game of charades involving a rubber chicken and a very confused vicar. Azrael, still trapped within the confines of the chipped teacup, observed it all with a mixture of weary amusement and a growing sense of opportunity.

His escape plan, hatched during a particularly enthusiastic rendition of "Twinkle Twinkle Little Star" (sung off-key, naturally), was audacious, bordering on reckless. It relied heavily on distraction, a pinch of poorly controlled magic, and the general mayhem that seemed to follow Agnes wherever she went.

First, he needed a distraction. Enter Princess Fluffybutt III. The chihuahua, mid-chase of a rogue crouton, had managed to ensnare herself in a particularly elaborate floral arrangement. The ensuing yips and frantic scrabbling provided the perfect cover. Azrael, using his dwindling magical reserves, subtly amplified the chihuahua's distress, creating a symphony of canine panic that drowned out all other conversation.

The vicar, bless his cotton socks, attempted to intervene, his attempts at rescuing the dog resulting in a spectacular entanglement of floral wire and clerical robes. The children, naturally, found this uproariously funny and joined in the chaos, creating a swirling vortex of tiny limbs, sugar cubes, and scattered tea sandwiches.

This was it, his moment. With the attention completely diverted, Azrael focused his remaining energy. He visualized a small crack, a fissure in the porcelain prison, a way out. The teacup vibrated, a faint tremor running through its delicate form. He concentrated, pushing with all his might, a grumpy genie's will focusing into a tiny magical explosion.

The crack widened. A sliver of light pierced the darkness. Then, with a satisfying *pop* , Azrael was free! He tumbled onto the tablecloth, landing with a soft *thump* amidst a sea of spilled tea and half-eaten biscuits.

He blinked, momentarily disoriented. The world swam into focus: a blur of frantic adults, giggling children, and a very sheepish vicar trying to untangle himself from a rose bush. Princess Fluffybutt III, now free from her floral confinement, was happily licking her paws, completely oblivious to the near-apocalyptic scene she'd orchestrated.

Agnes, however, noticed him. Or rather, she noticed the small, grumpy genie standing amidst the wreckage of her tea party. She didn't scream, surprisingly. She simply adjusted her spectacles and peered at him, a faint smile playing on her lips.

"Well, Azrael," she said, her voice calm amidst the chaos, "I must say, that was a rather dramatic exit. I do hope you haven't broken anything else."

Azrael, still slightly dizzy from the escape, managed a weak smile."Just my pride, perhaps," he admitted, dusting off his miniature waistcoat. "And possibly a few of your more delicate teacups. My apologies."

Agnes chuckled. "Don't worry about it. I have spares. Hundreds of spares. In fact, I believe I have one just the right size for you, should you decide to...retire" she trailed off, looking knowingly at him.

Azrael considered this. Another teacup? He shuddered at the thought. Yet, the chaos, the absurdity, the surprisingly endearing clumsiness of it all, had a strange allure. He'd been expecting a grand escape, a heroic leap into the sunset, a return to his supposed former glory. Instead, he'd gotten a chaotic tea party and a surprisingly understanding librarian.

"Perhaps," Azrael conceded, a hint of a smile on his face. "Perhaps a slightly less... enthusiastic tea party next time?"

Agnes beamed. "Perhaps," she agreed, already rummaging in a nearby cupboard for more teacups. "But the rubber chicken remains. It's a crucial element to our gatherings."

The vicar, finally free from his floral prison, offered a tentative, "Perhaps some less... vigorous games of charades?" His voice was muffled slightly by the lingering presence of rose thorns clinging to his collar.

The children, still energized by the sugar rush, started a spontaneous game of tag, weaving between the adults and narrowly avoiding tripping over the scattered remnants of the tea party. The chihuahua, meanwhile, began to bark excitedly at a stray crumb of a cake.

Azrael sighed. It seemed his retirement plans were on hold, indefinitely. But as he watched the chaotic scene unfold, a strange sense of peace settled over him. This was hardly the majestic, powerful genie existence he once envisioned. But this...this was strangely satisfying. This was home, at least for a while. After all, there was more tea to be drunk, more chaos to be experienced, and more surprisingly delightful company to be found amidst the stacks of books and the collection of novelty teacups. And somewhere in the midst of it all, he realized that perhaps he'd found a different kind of magic after all. A magic that wasn't about grand pronouncements or dazzling displays of power, but about the quiet joy of unexpected friendships, the absurdity of everyday life, and the strangely comforting chaos of a well-organized (or not so well-organized) tea party. And yes, maybe another attempt at getting that sparkly "Sir Gawain and the Green Knight" book, too. Perhaps that was the magic that made it all worth it.

As Agnes began to clear the table, muttering something about a slightly more controlled game plan next week (though that seemed doubtful given Princess Fluffybutt III's perpetually mischievous glint in her eye), Azrael felt a sense of calm settle over him. Maybe retirement wasn't on the cards after all. Maybe his destiny, or at least his current mildly comfortable existence, lay amidst the stacks of books and the surprisingly comforting chaos of Agnes

Periwinkle's unconventional tea parties. Maybe he'd even learn to appreciate the rubber chicken. Eventually. Perhaps. After a very long, very strong cup of tea.

The next day dawned bright and cheerful, a stark contrast to Azrael's previously gloomy outlook. He'd even managed to repair a few of the chipped teacups using a surprisingly effective combination of honey, glitter, and a very small amount of his waning magic. He found himself quite enjoying the quiet moments in the library, perching on a shelf amongst the dusty tomes, eavesdropping on Agnes's whispered conversations with particularly unruly patrons. He even started to develop a grudging respect for the rubber chicken, after witnessing its participation in an impromptu puppet show starring a particularly enthusiastic group of toddlers.

He spent his days exploring the nooks and crannies of the library, discovering secret passages, hidden collections of antique postcards, and an entire shelf dedicated to the history of the humble teabag. He learned the names of the local squirrels, the preferred napping spots of the resident tabby cat, and even managed to decipher the cryptic scribbles on Agnes's to-do list (mostly involving reshelving and the purchase of more novelty teacups). His life had become a rather unexpected adventure, far removed from his initial vision of genie-dom. But in this quiet corner of the library, nestled amongst the books and the teacups, he discovered a different kind of magic, a magic that was less about grand pronouncements and dazzling displays of power, and more about the quiet joy of unexpected friendship, the absurd charm of everyday life, and the comforting chaos of a truly unique tea party. And perhaps, just perhaps, he was starting to truly appreciate the peculiar charm of being a grumpy genie in a human world. The tea, he decided, was definitely the best part.

And so, Azrael's tale continued, not as a grand epic of genie heroism, but as a charmingly quirky chronicle of a mildly grumpy genie finding unexpected contentment in the most unlikely of places– a small, unassuming library, filled with extraordinary teacups and even more extraordinary people. His story, a testament to the unpredictable nature of life, and the surprisingly delightful magic hidden within the everyday chaos, would continue to unfold, one chaotic tea party at a time.

A Small Victory

The escape was less a grand, cinematic burst of magical energy and more a frantic scramble. It began, rather undramatically, with a rogue sugar cube. One particularly ambitious cube, propelled by the frenetic energy of a particularly hyperactive child named Timmy, had lodged itself perfectly in the tiny crack of the teacup's handle. This, to Azrael, was a revelation. It wasn't a glamorous solution, but it was a solution nonetheless.

With the precision of a seasoned escape artist (albeit one significantly smaller than average), Azrael used a stray crumb – a rather large, suspiciously chocolate-flavored crumb – as a lever. He pried, he pushed, he even muttered a few exasperated incantations that sounded suspiciously like complaints about the appalling lack of decent-sized sugar cubes in the magical realm.

Finally, with a satisfying *pop* , the handle gave way. Azrael tumbled out, landing with a soft thud on a particularly fluffy Persian cat – a far cry from the heroic, smoke-filled arrival he'd envisioned. The cat, whose name was apparently Reginald the Third, merely blinked slowly, unimpressed. The sugar cube, however, seemed quite pleased with its contribution to the day's events.

Freedom, Azrael discovered, wasn't exactly the blissful experience he'd imagined. It was...sticky. The combination of sugar, tea residue, and cat fur created a rather unpleasant coating on his already frayed nerves. He felt like a miniature, disgruntled gingerbread man who'd spent too long rolling around in a sugar bowl.

He surveyed the battlefield, or rather, the tea-stained tablecloth. The aftermath of the tea party was a scene of utter chaos. Princess Fluffybutt III had successfully conquered a plate of cucumber sandwiches, leaving a trail of shredded napkin in her wake. The vicar, still sporting a rubber chicken hat, was attempting to explain quantum physics to a group of fascinated squirrels. Timmy, the sugar cube champion, was engaged in a spirited debate with a particularly grumpy-looking goldfish.

"Right," Azrael muttered, brushing cat fur from his...well, from wherever genies have fur. "Time to go. And never, ever, under any circumstances, to attend another tea party."

He attempted a dignified exit, but was promptly thwarted by Agnes, the librarian, who appeared carrying a dustpan and broom and wearing an expression that suggested she was considering adding'genie wrangling' to her already extensive list of job duties.

"Oh, Azrael, there you are! I was wondering where you'd gotten to. The children insisted you were hiding in the teapot, but I never believed them. It seemed terribly unlikely." Agnes' tone suggested that while she found the entire situation absurd, she somehow accepted it as another Tuesday afternoon at the library.

Azrael merely sighed. He had, after all, just survived a miniature genie sized sugar-cube fuelled tea party. What was one more slightly incredulous librarian? He even managed a weak smile.

"Unlikely, indeed," he conceded, attempting to regain some semblance of his usual (mildly grumpy) composure. "I've had... a rather eventful afternoon."

Agnes, never one to miss an opportunity for a good story, proceeded to engage him in a detailed account of the day's events, peppered with vivid descriptions of Timmy's sugar-cube-launching techniques and the vicar's surprisingly eloquent interpretation of Schrödinger's cat using a rubber chicken. Azrael listened patiently, realizing that escaping the teacup had only delayed the inevitable. Humans, it seemed, had a remarkable ability to turn even the most extraordinary events into excruciatingly mundane conversations.

He decided to escape again, but this time with a plan. He would use the library's vast collection of books to his advantage. Specifically, he would use the book of advanced genie conjuring spells – a book he'd accidentally stumbled upon during his initial capture. He had a feeling he'd need all the advanced conjuring he could muster. His current magical reserves were alarmingly low, depleted by the constant struggle to maintain some modicum of control amidst the chaos.

Finding the book proved easier than anticipated. Agnes, after a lengthy description of Reginald the Third's fondness for tuna, inadvertently pointed him in the right direction. He'd left the book precisely where he'd found it, nestled among the dusty tomes on medieval alchemy.

The spell was complicated, involving a series of hand gestures that resembled a particularly frantic game of charades and incantations that sounded like a disgruntled badger attempting to recite Shakespeare. He had to maintain the precise concentration of chamomile tea fumes, ensuring the exact humidity level, while simultaneously avoiding eye contact with a particularly inquisitive praying mantis that had somehow appeared on the shelf.

Finally, with a flourish that was more stumble than style, the spell worked. A shimmering portal opened, not with a glorious burst of light, but with a soft *poof*, like a deflated balloon.

"Well, this is certainly underwhelming," Azrael grumbled as he stepped through. He expected a grand, celestial escape, perhaps even a ride on a magical unicorn. Instead, he found himself in a rather ordinary-looking broom cupboard.

"Are you alright, sir?" a voice croaked from the darkness. It belonged to the library's janitor, a rather portly man with a surprisingly cheerful disposition, despite his obvious discomfort at discovering a tiny genie in his broom cupboard.

Azrael sighed. This was clearly not the grand finale he'd envisioned. Perhaps retirement wasn't such a bad idea after all. Maybe he'd retire to a dimension where tea parties didn't involve runaway chihuahuas, miniature genies, or an overabundance of sugar cubes. A dimension, perhaps, where even the janitor possessed a modicum of surprise at encountering a genie in a broom cupboard. A dimension where he could simply exist without encountering such calamitous events. Yes, retirement sounded much, much better.

But then again, the janitor offered him a surprisingly good cup of tea. And it didn't involve sugar cubes. Perhaps, just perhaps, there was still hope for Azrael, even in the midst of the ever-present chaos of the human world. Perhaps even a slightly less grumpy existence was within reach. Perhaps. Just perhaps. The thought lingered, as sweet and unexpected as the tea itself. He decided to take another sip, his previous vow of never attending another tea party slowly, tentatively wavering. This time, he thought, perhaps he could use the sugar-cube launching skills he acquired during the teacup incident to his advantage. The journey to a less grumpy existence was likely to be bumpy and chaotic, but at least it held a hint of delicious possibilities. He smiled, a genuine, ungrumpy smile, as the warmth of the tea spread through his tiny, exhausted frame. Maybe, just maybe, life as a genie wasn't so bad after all. The adventure, it turned out, had only just begun.

Philosophical Pigeons

The pigeons, oh, the pigeons. They were not your average, run-of-the-mill, pecking-at-crumbs pigeons. No, these were philosophical pigeons, imbued with an unsettling level of intellectual curiosity and a frankly alarming penchant for brie. Summoned inadvertently by the self-help guru's unintentionally potent positive affirmations –a detail I still find utterly infuriating – they were now my problem. My *very* significant problem.

They'd settled on my balcony, a feathered flock of existential angst, demanding not just seed, but Socratic dialogues. One particularly pompous pigeon, a particularly plump fellow with a distinctly superior air, insisted on debating the merits of Sartre versus Camus while delicately nibbling a wedge of cheddar. It was, to put it mildly, a surreal experience.

My attempts at reason were, as usual, met with spectacular failure. I tried diplomacy – offering them an unlimited supply of the finest birdseed, a veritable buffet of sunflower seeds, millet, and cracked corn. They eyed my offering with disdain. "Birdseed?" scoffed the leader, a creature I'd begun to refer to internally as "Professor Pouter." "Such pedestrian fare! We demand Gouda, and a discourse on the nature of being!"

Their demands escalated. First it was the Gouda, then came the request for a selection of fine wines – a vintage Pinot Grigio, if I recall correctly, was high on the list. Then they started demanding caviar. Caviar! For pigeons! I found myself frantically searching my surprisingly extensive magical inventory, more accustomed to locating lost socks than high-end delicacies.

The situation reached its apex – or perhaps its nadir, depending on your perspective – during what I can only describe as the Great Cheese Caper. Led by Professor Pouter, the philosophical flock decided that a simple supermarket raid was the only solution to their culinary crisis. I watched in horror – and a touch of grudging admiration – as they orchestrated a daring heist, utilising their surprisingly adept teamwork and miniature beaks to plunder the dairy aisle. It was a symphony of squawks, flapping wings, and the clatter of cheese tumbling to the floor.

The supermarket security guard, bless his cotton socks, was entirely overwhelmed. He was a stout fellow, but not exactly equipped to deal with a highly organized flock of philosophy-quoting pigeons who treated the theft of artisanal cheese as a philosophical experiment. He chased them around, arms flailing, looking like a particularly flustered gamekeeper in a slapstick comedy. I considered intervening, but honestly, watching his hopeless attempts at apprehending them provided a certain grim satisfaction.

The ensuing chaos was, of course, caught on camera. Within hours, the PigeonPhilosophers hashtag was trending, and the videos of the Great Cheese Caper went viral. News outlets from around the world were reporting on the incident, speculating on the intellectual capabilities of the pigeons and their refined taste in cheese. I, the disgruntled genie responsible for their existence, was not mentioned. A small victory, I suppose.

My attempts at damage control were, again, less than effective. I tried to negotiate a truce, offering a lifetime supply of the finest birdseed, a comfortable pigeon condo, and the promise to never, ever, summon a self-help guru again. They considered this offer –seriously considered it – before rejecting it with a series of knowing coos and eloquent squawks.

It turned out they weren't simply after the cheese. They were after the *experience* . The thrill of the heist, the notoriety, the sheer absurdity of it all. They'd become minor celebrities, their philosophical debates punctuated by the occasional snippet of supermarket security footage. They even started demanding interviews with avian-focused journalists, their intellectual pronouncements delivered with a remarkable degree of avian eloquence.

The climax of this whole ridiculous affair came during a late-night debate about the inherent contradictions of free will versus determinism. They were perched on the edge of a rather prestigious fountain, surrounded by a growing audience of enthralled onlookers. Professor Pouter, mid-sentence, suddenly dropped a crumb of brie. He paused, looked at the crumb, then at the audience, and delivered a final, pithy pronouncement: "The existential angst of a fallen crumb is profound indeed."

Then they flew off into the night, leaving behind a bewildered crowd and a city that had officially embraced the philosophical pigeon phenomenon. I sighed, slumped back against my balcony railing, and reached for a bottle of something strong. It wasn't just the philosophical pigeons or their cheese-fueled rampages that wore me out, it was the sheer, unadulterated absurdity of the whole situation. Retirement really seemed like a good idea. Just as long as there were no sentient teacups in my new dimension. Teacups were easily as troublesome as philosophy-obsessed pigeons, or perhaps even more so. The thought of another tea party sent a shiver down my spine. And this time, even the finest Gouda wouldn't be enough to alleviate the stress. This genie needed a vacation, and a very strong cup of something significantly less volcanic than my earlier attempts at brewing tea. Perhaps a nice herbal infusion. Yes, that sounded significantly less problematic. And perhaps, just perhaps, a dimension devoid of cheese-loving, philosophical birds.

The next morning, however, as I prepared for my planned escape, I found a small package on my balcony. Inside was a single, perfectly formed wheel of brie, accompanied by a tiny, handwritten note that simply read, "With our compliments, from your friends, the Pigeon Philosophers." Well, I thought, I should probably get some crackers. Retirement would have to wait. At least until I'd worked out a way to make those pigeons disappear. Or perhaps found a way to successfully negotiate with them about a more sensible, cheese-free diet. The challenge was definitely an intriguing one. And as a genie, a rather grumpy, underpowered one, I found myself compelled to take up the challenge. After all, what kind of a genie would I be if I simply gave up on my avian tormentors? I wasn't quite ready to join a quiet, cheese-less retirement just yet. Besides, a little chaos was rather invigorating. As long as it didn't involve any more reality TV appearances or accidentally summoning sentient teacups. The pigeons, while a source of ongoing frustration, were, at least, predictable in their chaos. I knew what to expect. I knew the rules of engagement. It was in fact, a rather comforting thought.

Negotiating with Pigeons

My initial attempts at negotiation were, shall we say, less than successful. I tried reason. I explained, in what I considered to be perfectly clear and concise terms, that a diet consisting primarily of brie was not only unhealthy for them but also incredibly inconvenient for me. Their response was a chorus of cooing laughter – a sound I found remarkably irritating, especially given the sheer volume of it.

"But the brie," one particularly plump pigeon, who I mentally dubbed Bartholomew, declared with a philosophical air, "is the cornerstone of our intellectual pursuits. It inspires our musings, fuels our debates, and provides the necessary calcium for the sharpest of pigeon minds."

I blinked. "Calcium? From brie? Bartholomew, my feathered friend, you are basing your intellectual prowess on a fundamentally flawed understanding of nutrition."

This prompted a flurry of indignant coos and the flapping of several hundred wings, a cacophony that nearly blew my rather expensive (and surprisingly difficult to acquire) fez clean off my head. I considered resorting to magic, but the last time I'd attempted a significant spell – a simple vanishing act for a particularly persistent chihuahua – it had resulted in the chihuahua morphing briefly into a potted fern before reverting to its original, yipping form, but with an uncanny resemblance to Albert Einstein. I wasn't eager to repeat that experience, especially not with a flock of brie-obsessed intellectual pigeons.

My next strategy involved bribery. I offered them sunflower seeds, a staple of any self-respecting pigeon's diet. They looked at me with disdain. "Sunflower seeds?" Bartholomew cooed, wrinkling his beak in disgust. "Dreadfully pedestrian. Uninspired. Lacking in that certain je ne sais quoi that only a fine triple-crème brie can provide."

I sighed. I was running out of options, and my supplies of brie were dwindling alarmingly. I attempted a different tack. I tried appealing to their intellectual curiosity. I spoke to them about the finer points of avian aerodynamics, the subtle nuances of philosophical debate, even the complex mathematics involved in calculating the optimal trajectory for a perfectly thrown crumb. They listened with rapt attention – until I mentioned that all this intellectual exertion could be negatively impacted by their excessive brie consumption. The outraged squawking that followed nearly shattered my eardrums.

Clearly, a different approach was needed. I decided to delve into their philosophical pursuits, figuring I could use their own arguments against them. I'd observed their debates – fascinatingly incoherent, but still debates. Their intellectual arguments revolved around the existential nature of crumbs, the ethics of scavenging, and the philosophical implications of different types of bread.

"I understand your intellectual curiosity," I began, trying to adopt a more conciliatory tone. "But wouldn't a broader range of philosophical subjects be... more enriching? Consider the works of Nietzsche, for example, or the profound wisdom of Confucius. Think of the intellectual stimulation!"

Bartholomew tilted his head, considering my words. "Nietzsche? Confucius? Never heard of them. Have they written on the existential dilemma of the perfectly ripened brie?"

I groaned inwardly. This was going nowhere fast. I needed a new tactic, a grand strategic maneuver. Perhaps something... theatrical.

I cleared my throat dramatically. "My dear pigeon philosophers," I announced, striking a pose I'd seen a particularly flamboyant magician use once – a rather unfortunate incident involving a disappearing rabbit and a very startled audience. "I propose a challenge! A contest of intellects! If you can answer my philosophical question to my satisfaction, I shall provide you with an endless supply of... well, not brie. But something almost as good."

They were intrigued. Bartholomew puffed out his chest. "Very well, genie. Pose your question."

I took a deep breath, steeling myself for whatever ludicrous response I was about to receive. "What," I declared, with as much gravitas as I could muster, "is the sound of one hand clapping?"

The pigeons erupted in a cacophony of squawks, wings flapping wildly. They debated, they argued, they cooed and they squabbled. The philosophical implications of a single clapping hand obviously sparked more intense debate than I had anticipated.

Hours passed. The sun set, painting the sky in hues of orange and purple. The pigeons, exhausted but undeterred, continued their passionate, if slightly unhinged, discussion. I secretly began to suspect this might be a fool's errand. My attempt at a Zen koan had apparently unleashed a storm of avian philosophical debate. They were completely oblivious to the fact that I was hoping this would distract them from their brie obsession.

Finally, just as I was about to concede defeat, Bartholomew, looking utterly ruffled and slightly dishevelled, stepped forward. "We have reached a consensus," he announced, his voice raspy from hours of intense debate. "The sound of one hand clapping is... the sound of utter silence punctuated by the faintest whisper of existential dread."

I stared at him, utterly speechless. It was... surprisingly insightful. Not what I expected, certainly, but insightful nonetheless.

I decided then and there to make a deal. I would provide them with an alternative to brie: a lifetime supply of the finest, most ethically sourced, and, dare I say it, intellectually stimulating sunflower seeds. In exchange, they would agree to limit their brie consumption to special occasions, like, say, the annual philosophical symposium on the ethics of crumb acquisition.

They agreed, surprisingly readily. Perhaps the existential dread of a brie-less existence was a more compelling argument than I'd initially thought. And just like that, the pigeon problem, for now at least, was solved. Though I suspected my quiet, cheese-less retirement was still a long way off. The universe, as I was rapidly learning, had a penchant for unexpected philosophical debates, whether they involved genies, pigeons, or the existential dread of a single, clapping hand. I wasn't sure I was up for the next challenge, but then again, what kind of a genie would I be if I let a little philosophical chaos get in the way of my (eventually) well-deserved retirement? The quest for a cheese-free existence continued. One sunflower seed at a time.

The Great Cheese Caper

The treaty, fragile as a week-old éclair, held for precisely seventeen minutes. Seventeen minutes of blissful, cheese-free serenity, during which I almost dared to believe that my retirement dreams weren't entirely pipe dreams made of cheddar. Then, the cooing resumed. It wasn't the gentle, almost melodic cooing of contentment; this was a cacophony, a feathered symphony of avarice.

It began with a single pigeon, a particularly plump fellow with an unnervingly intelligent glint in his beady eye. He landed on the windowsill, his tiny claws clicking against the glass, and proceeded to tap a single, tiny sunflower seed against the pane. This wasn't a request. This was a demand. I sighed, the sound echoing in the surprisingly spacious confines of my rather underwhelming genie abode (a slightly damp cupboard under the stairs, if I'm being brutally honest).

More pigeons arrived, their numbers swelling like a particularly aggressive yeast infection. Soon, my windowsill resembled a feathered, cooing parliament, each member pecking insistently at the glass, their collective gaze burning a hole in my already frayed nerves. The sunflower seed offering was quickly upgraded to demands for larger, more substantial provisions. Crackers, then bread crumbs, then... cheese. Yes, cheese. The very thing I had so painstakingly avoided.

My carefully constructed plan for a cheese-free existence crumbled faster than a poorly baked soufflé. These weren't your average city pigeons; these were organised crime, feathered and flapping. They had a hierarchy, a pecking order (pun intended, and I deeply regret it), and a surprisingly sophisticated understanding of logistics. Their leader, a particularly bold specimen with a single, slightly askew feather atop his head, seemed to be orchestrating the whole operation with chilling efficiency.

"Right then," I muttered, rubbing my temples. "Round two it is."

Negotiations proved as fruitful as attempting to extract sunshine from a cucumber. They didn't want sunflower seeds. They didn't want crackers. They craved cheese. And not just any cheese. They demanded *Camembert*. Camembert! The audacity! The sheer, unadulterated cheese-based chutzpah!

My escape from the previous cheese-related catastrophe had been a close call. The idea of facing another, this time potentially involving a supermarket raid by a highly organized flock of avian cheese aficionados, filled me with a profound sense of dread. Retirement, in a cheese-free dimension, felt further away than ever.

The next morning dawned with a flurry of feathered wings and a whole lot of squawking. My little cupboard became a staging ground for the Great Cheese Caper. The leader pigeon, whom I'd secretly nicknamed "Cheesebeard" (don't judge me, it fit), had drawn up a detailed map, meticulously crafted from tiny, stolen scraps of newspaper. I was forced to admire its precision, even as I worried about the implications of a pigeon-led heist.

The supermarket was a chaotic whirlwind of activity. Cheesebeard, with his team of perfectly trained pigeon accomplices, orchestrated a dazzling display of avian acrobatics. They zipped through the aisles, their tiny beaks expertly selecting wheels of Camembert, Gouda, and even a rather expensive wedge of Stilton. They avoided security cameras with remarkable agility, their flight paths so precise they could make a seasoned Navy SEAL blush.

The sheer audacity of it all was almost comical. I watched, half-amused and half-terrified, as the pigeons loaded their spoils onto a miniature trolley they'd somehow managed to commandeer. The whole scene played out like a slapstick heist movie, except with considerably more squawking and less suave sophistication.

Things got messy. A small child, witnessing this unparalleled scene of avian larceny, shrieked with delight. A security guard, initially confused, quickly became utterly overwhelmed by the sheer number of pigeons swarming around him, flapping their wings and creating a feathered vortex of cheese-related mayhem. Chaos reigned supreme.

The pigeons escaped with a considerable amount of stolen dairy, disappearing into the sunset – or rather, the rapidly darkening twilight – with a collective chirp of triumph. I, meanwhile, was left standing amidst the wreckage of the cheese aisle, feeling a strange mixture of grudging admiration and utter exhaustion.

The aftermath involved a lengthy interrogation by a surprisingly understanding police officer (who seemed more amused than annoyed by the whole affair), a large bill for the supermarket, and several very uncomfortable conversations with my (now very worried) landlord.

The following days were a blur of explaining, cleaning, and attempting to negotiate a new treaty with Cheesebeard and his increasingly demanding flock. The demand was no longer just cheese; they now insisted on gourmet crackers, seed mixes, and small, exquisitely crafted pigeon houses. My retirement, it seemed, was further away than ever. I'd underestimated the ambition, the organizational skills, and the sheer, unbridled love of cheese possessed by a highly organized flock of city pigeons.

But I was a genie, after all. Even a grumpy, slightly incompetent one. And if there was one thing I'd learned in my tenure as a magical wish-granter, it was this: you never, ever underestimate the power of cheese, especially when combined with the cunning of a particularly well-organized group of pigeons. Retirement was still on the cards, but now I was seriously considering adding a clause to my magical contract: "No pigeons. Absolutely no pigeons." The universe, however, remained determined to test this resolve. I had a sneaking suspicion that this particular chapter in my life, filled with feathered bandits and stolen cheeses, was only just beginning.

The following week saw an unexpected development. News reports started appearing about a string of daring robberies, not involving cheese, but priceless gemstones. The suspects? A gang known only as the "Feathered Fiends." The description of their modus operandi bore an uncanny resemblance to the cheese heist, only with sapphires and rubies replacing Camembert and Cheddar.

I stared at the newspaper photo – a grainy shot of a pigeon with an

askew feather, looking remarkably like Cheesebeard, perched atop a skyscraper. My jaw dropped. It suddenly all made sense. The cheese had been a distraction, a training exercise. The true goal had always been far greater. My quiet, cheese-less retirement was a distant dream. Instead, I was now embroiled in a far more significant and significantly less cheesy problem: an international jewel heist
perpetrated by a highly organized flock of avian masterminds. Perhaps a quiet life wasn't in the cards after all. Perhaps I needed a new career – perhaps a consultant for high-end security systems. Or perhaps, just perhaps, a change of dimension. The possibilities, even in the absence of cheese, were surprisingly vast. One thing was for sure: this was going to be a long, and very interesting, retirement.

And I would not be surprised if the next demand involved, not cheese, but a small, exquisitely crafted diamond tiara, for
Cheesebeard, naturally. After all, a boss needed proper headwear.

The following months were a blur of international travel, high-speed chases, and very uncomfortable encounters with various authorities. I learned to appreciate the intricate workings of various alarm systems, the importance of silent flight, and the astonishing ability of pigeons to navigate complex urban landscapes. They were surprisingly resourceful, these feathered fiends. And astonishingly well-dressed. Many of them seemed to favor little tiny tuxedos. I wouldn't lie, they were quite dashing.

In the end, the Feathered Fiends were apprehended, but not before they'd managed to pull off one last, spectacular heist— a daring raid on a renowned museum, resulting in the disappearance of a legendary golden egg, the size of a small car. News reports suggested that the egg had mysteriously been replaced with a single, perfectly formed wheel of Camembert. A fitting end, I thought, to the Great Cheese Caper. A masterpiece of avian
ingenuity, audacious planning and utterly baffling cheese-related motives. I'd finally managed to secure a well-deserved, if slightly delayed, retirement, far away from the chaos of inept humans and cunning pigeons. And, naturally, cheese. Lots and lots of cheese.

The universe, it seemed, had a strange sense of humor. And a bottomless supply of cheese. The next chapter, I hoped, would be cheese-free. But I wasn't holding my breath.

Pigeon Diplomacy

My retirement, it turned out, was less a tranquil escape and more a temporary reprieve. The universe, clearly a fan of cosmic slapstick, had other plans. My peaceful existence, envisioned as a sun-drenched hammock swaying gently in a cheese-free breeze, was rudely interrupted by the unmistakable sound of... cooing. Not the gentle, romantic cooing of lovebirds, oh no. This was a chorus of indignant squawks, a feathered frenzy of flapping wings and frankly, quite aggressive pecking.

The pigeons were back. Not just any pigeons, mind you. These were the descendants of the Great Cheese Caper crew, inheriting not only their ancestors' audacious spirit but also their baffling obsession with dairy products. They'd reformed, naturally, under a new, surprisingly well-organized leadership structure (apparently, pigeon society is far more complex than I'd initially assumed). Their demands were, as ever, both unreasonable and oddly specific. They wanted, and I quote, "a monument to the glorious history of pigeon-kind, crafted from the finest Gruyère."

I sighed. Retirement was proving to be more demanding than summoning a decent cup of tea. The Gruyère request was particularly galling; my current financial situation involved precisely zero Gruyère, and frankly, a rather substantial debt to a rather irritated cheese wholesaler. Negotiation was clearly in order.

Diplomacy, even if it involved dealing with exceptionally demanding birds. This wasn't exactly the "far, far away from inept humans" retirement package I'd envisioned. These feathered fiends, it seemed, were the ultimate test of my newly acquired patience.

My first attempt involved a carefully crafted speech, delivered with what I hoped was an air of regal authority. I cleared my throat, puffed out my nonexistent chest, and began: "My feathered friends," I announced, attempting a tone of benevolent leadership, "I understand your desire for a Gruyère monument. However, I must point out that such an undertaking presents certain... logistical challenges." The pigeons responded with a coordinated barrage of droppings. Diplomacy, apparently, was not their forte.

Plan B involved bribery. I spent an uncomfortable afternoon trawling through local pet stores, acquiring an assortment of birdseed that would make a small bird sanctuary blush. Sunflowers seeds, millet, cracked corn – I even splurged on some exotic niger seeds. The sheer quantity of birdseed could probably feed a small flock for a year. I laid out my offering, a veritable mountain of avian delicacies. My hope was that they would find this distraction compelling enough to forget the Gruyère monument. I watched as the leader, a particularly plump pigeon with a rather imperious glint in his eye, surveyed the scene. He pecked thoughtfully at a sunflower seed, then looked up at me, his expression inscrutable.

"Birdseed?" he finally squawked, his voice surprisingly deep for such a small creature. "You think mere birdseed will appease the glorious descendants of the Great Cheese Caper? You underestimate our refined palates!"

I stared at the defiant pigeon. My carefully crafted plan had failed miserably. My attempts at peace had met with a peckish rejection.

These were not just ordinary pigeons; these were philosophical pigeons, existentialist pigeons, possibly even postmodernist pigeons.

It was clear a different approach was needed. A more...philosophical approach.

"Alright," I conceded, my voice laced with a hint of defeat.

"Birdseed is not enough. Let's talk about the philosophy of Gruyère. The existential dread of a life devoid of cheese... I get it. The quest for the ultimate dairy delight... I understand the implications. But tell me, my feathered friends, is a monument really the answer?"

The pigeons looked at each other, a flurry of head bobs and wing-flicks indicating a serious discussion was underway. I pressed on, feeling a strange sense of confidence as I went deeper into my impromptu philosophy lecture for pigeons. "Consider the ephemeral nature of cheese! Its delicate flavor, its short lifespan! Must we immortalize it in a monument of stone and Gruyère? Or is there a more... fluid, a more ephemeral approach? A life less ordinary, as it were."

One particularly intellectual-looking pigeon, adorned with an unusually shiny feather, seemed to be pondering my words. He cocked his head, then let out a series of coos that sounded suspiciously like agreement. He hopped forward and pecked at the pile of birdseed. Soon, other pigeons joined him, a flurry of feathers and pecking in a surprisingly harmonious display.

"Very well," the leader announced after a moment, his voice surprisingly conciliatory. "We accept your...philosophical proposal. Unlimited birdseed. And the occasional philosophical discussion. But," he added with a mischievous glint in his eye, "we reserve the right to occasionally raid for cheese. It's a matter of principle, you understand."

And so, the Pigeon Treaty of Gruyère was signed, sealed, and delivered (mostly through intense staring and the strategic placement of birdseed). My retirement remained slightly less tranquil than planned, but at least there was a clear protocol now. Unlimited birdseed in exchange for the occasional philosophical debate and the inevitable, yet somehow acceptable, raids on local cheese shops. It wasn't exactly the quiet life I'd imagined, but at least it was... interesting. And, remarkably, cheese-free, for the most part. For now. The universe, I suspected, was still plotting something, probably involving cheese. But hey, at least I had the birdseed. And that, my friends, is a victory in itself.

The days that followed were a bizarre dance between philosophical discussions with particularly eloquent pigeons and the constant replenishment of my birdseed supply. It became a ritual. I'd find the leader and his flock on my doorstep early in the morning, always awaiting my next philosophical point on existentialism or the nature of reality. Their intellect truly surprised me, often pointing out flaws in my logic with more cunning and precision than I'd encountered from some human philosophers. Our talks would range from the absurdity of human existence to the merits of different types of birdseed (apparently, niger seeds are highly overrated).

Once, during a particularly lively discussion on the ethics of cheese consumption, a stray cat attempted to ambush the flock. It became a chaotic scene of flapping wings, squawks, and the cat's rather undignified retreat after a rather vigorous pecking from the leader.

It was a testament to their resilience, their intellect, and their ability to defend their territory (and their unlimited supply of birdseed). It was a surprisingly harmonious existence and an experience I would have never imagined during my previous, rather less avian-centric existence.

The occasional cheese raid still occurred. I wouldn't lie, and say I didn't feel a twinge of irritation when I saw news reports of another cheese heist. But I'd learned to simply accept it as part of the package. They would return with tales of daring exploits, often punctuated with philosophical musings on the taste of different cheeses, leading to some of the most peculiar yet intriguing discussions I'd ever had. After all, what's retirement without a bit of feathered chaos and a whole lot of philosophical pigeon-based discourse? Besides, I'd found a great cheese supplier that offered discounts for bulk purchases. Let the games continue.

A Truce of Sorts

The largest of the pigeons, a portly fellow I'd started calling Bartholomew, puffed out his chest, a collection of iridescent feathers shimmering in the afternoon sun. He cleared his throat, a sound like gravel gargling with buttermilk. "Right then, Azrael," he declared, his voice surprisingly deep for such a small creature, "we've reached a... a compromise, shall we say?"

I raised an eyebrow, skeptical. These weren't exactly the most reliable negotiators. Their philosophical discussions often devolved into squabbles over crumbs, and their concept of "compromise" usually involved me supplying more cheese.

"A truce, if you will," Bartholomew continued, seemingly sensing my doubts. "We'll cease our... er... *spirited* debates on the existential nature of brie right here in your... well, your *domain* ." He gestured vaguely at my somewhat dilapidated gazebo, now adorned with an impressive collection of pigeon droppings.

"And in exchange?" I prompted, my voice dripping with weary anticipation.

Bartholomew looked at me with what I could only describe as a pigeon-like version of a sly grin. "Cheese," he stated simply. "A regular supply of high-quality cheddar. And perhaps, occasionally, a sliver of that... what was it you called it... Gruyère?"

Gruyère. The very thought sent shivers of deliciousness down my spine. It was an exquisite cheese, its nutty flavor a far cry from the usual cheddar these feathered philosophers seemed to favor. Still, a truce was a truce. My ears were still ringing from their last debate on the merits of Camembert versus Gouda, a philosophical duel that had involved a near-miss with a rather aggressive wing-slap to my face.

"Fine," I conceded, sighing inwardly. "Cheddar, and a *very* occasional sliver of Gruyère. But that's the final offer. No more philosophical debates about cheese within a five-mile radius of this gazebo. Understood?"

A chorus of squawks, this time more of agreement than indignant outrage, filled the air. Bartholomew, clearly the leader of this feathered flock, nodded decisively. "Agreed. However," he added, a mischievous glint in his beady eye, "our philosophical discussions will continue. Merely... elsewhere. We've been considering a new location – the town square. The acoustics are rather superb there, you see."

I suppressed a groan. The town square. That meant I would be subjected to their endless debates on the merits of various cheeses – from afar, yes, but still within earshot. It was a small victory, but a victory nonetheless. I had managed to relocate their philosophical conclaves, albeit to a place where they would probably attract an audience. This could, I mused, be a disaster of epic proportions, perhaps ending up in a viral video on the internet. I shuddered at the thought.

"Very well," I conceded, "But if I hear even one squawk about the texture of Stilton before noon, the Gruyère supply is cut off."

Bartholomew bobbed his head vigorously. "Understood, Azrael. Understood. Now, about that cheese..."

The ensuing negotiations over the specific types of cheese, the delivery schedule, and the appropriate level of humidity for optimal cheese preservation, proved far more complex than I'd anticipated. Bartholomew, it turned out, was a surprisingly shrewd negotiator. He argued passionately for the inclusion of artisanal cheeses, citing their "complex philosophical underpinnings," a term he seemed to apply liberally to any cheese with an unusual texture or smell.

After what felt like an eternity (though it was probably only about an hour), we finally reached a mutually acceptable agreement. The pigeons would receive a weekly supply of cheddar, with a monthly allocation of Gruyère (the quantity strictly limited to prevent overindulgence, and the associated philosophical ramifications). In return, they would conduct their intellectual discussions beyond the five-mile radius, with a special exemption for one "cheese-tasting seminar" per quarter, held – naturally – in my gazebo.

As I watched the pigeons waddle away, their bellies full of cheddar and their minds abuzz with impending philosophical debates, I felt a strange sense of... peace. It wasn't the tranquil, cheese-free nirvana I had originally envisioned for my retirement, but it was... manageable. Besides, I had a feeling that these feathered philosophers were going to provide me with an endless source of amusement, if nothing else. Perhaps retirement wouldn't be so bad after all. As long as I kept a good supply of Gruyère on hand.

The following weeks were a strange blend of quiet contemplation and chaotic bursts of philosophical squawking emanating from the town square. The pigeons, true to their word, largely stayed away from my gazebo, though the occasional stray feather would land on my sun lounger, a subtle reminder of their presence. Their debates, as relayed by the townsfolk (who were, to put it mildly, bewildered by the avian intellectualism), were a fascinating blend of philosophical pondering and surprisingly astute cheese criticism.

One particular debate, overheard by a local journalist and later published in the town newspaper, centered around the question of whether the "subtle tang of aged cheddar" was a sign of superior quality or merely a consequence of improper storage. The debate had apparently lasted for three hours and involved several elaborate avian dances, concluding with a unanimous agreement that further research was required. The newspaper article concluded with a quote from Bartholomew: "The quest for the perfect cheese is, after all, a lifelong journey." I couldn't help but chuckle.

My retirement wasn't exactly what I'd planned, but it was certainly... interesting. The pigeons were unpredictable, their philosophical excursions occasionally bordering on the absurd, but their company, in its own peculiar way, had grown on me. They brought a certain... zest to my otherwise peaceful (or rather, previously peaceful) existence.

The quarterly cheese-tasting seminars proved to be equally entertaining. The pigeons, dressed in miniature chef's hats (a whimsical addition by Bartholomew, apparently inspired by a discarded magazine), would present their findings with a seriousness that was both hilarious and endearing. They'd analyze the texture, the aroma, the aftertaste, with the intensity of seasoned sommeliers. Their pronouncements, delivered with the most dramatic of pigeon squawks, were often peppered with unexpected insights into the human condition, surprisingly profound statements delivered amidst the munching of cheese.

One particular tasting session focused on a rather pungent variety of Roquefort. Bartholomew, after a lengthy and dramatic sniff, proclaimed, "The scent, Azrael, is a metaphor for the complexities of life itself. Strong, pungent, yet undeniably... delicious." I couldn't help but agree. The pigeons, even with their occasional cheese-fueled philosophical ramblings, had a knack for finding unexpected meaning in the simplest things, a trait I found both endearing and rather inspiring.

My retirement with the pigeons wasn't tranquil, certainly not cheese-free, but it was an unexpected adventure, a comedic symphony of squawks, cheese, and surprisingly profound philosophical musings. And, I had to admit, it was a far cry from the humdrum existence I had initially envisioned. Maybe retirement wasn't so bad after all. Maybe, just maybe, the universe knew what it was doing after all, even if its methods were a little unconventional, a little messy, and involved an awful lot of cheese. As long as the cheese was of good quality, I was content.

Viral Fame

The flickering screen of my borrowed smartphone – a rather pathetic attempt at blending in with the modern human – displayed my face, magnified to monstrous proportions, amidst a whirlwind of poorly-edited footage and shrieking commentary. It was a scene of culinary chaos, a reality TV show cooking competition gone spectacularly wrong. Or, as I preferred to think of it, a blatant disregard for basic genie etiquette. Me, Azrael, the mildly grumpy genie of considerably less-than-advertised magical prowess, was viral.

The initial incident, which involved a misplaced soufflé, a spontaneous rain of glitter, and a rather startled celebrity chef, had apparently resonated with the collective human psyche. The show's producers, bless their clueless hearts, had edited the footage with a peculiar blend of dramatic music and slow-motion replays, transforming my exasperated sighs and involuntary magical hiccups into a compelling narrative of "mystical mayhem." The hashtag HairyGenie was trending. I groaned inwardly.

My attempts at maintaining a low profile had been about as successful as a snowball fight in the Sahara. Every attempt to leave my temporary lodgings – a rather dingy motel room on the outskirts of some forgotten town – was thwarted by a swarm of paparazzi, their flashbulbs blinding, their questions intrusive. "What's your secret to that amazing glitter effect, Hairy Genie?" one particularly persistent reporter had asked, his voice dripping with saccharine enthusiasm. I'd responded with a withering glare and a magically-induced nosebleed. Apparently, that made for excellent television as well.

The interview requests flooded my inbox – or rather, the inbox of the temporary human-issued email address I'd begrudgingly acquired. "The Today Show," "Good Morning America," even that horrifyingly cheerful morning show with the overly-caffeinated host– they all wanted a piece of the "Hairy Genie" pie. I considered hiding in a teacup again. It wasn't particularly comfortable, but it offered a certain degree of anonymity.

The fan mail was, if anything, even worse. Requests for autographed teacups (ironic, considering my history with them), demands for personalized glitter showers, and heartfelt letters from individuals who identified deeply with my "mystical struggles"filled the overflowing mailbox. One particularly zealous admirer had sent me a knitted version of myself, complete with miniature, poorly-stitched fez. I shuddered.

Managing this sudden surge of unwanted attention was proving to be far more challenging than fending off a swarm of overly-enthusiastic self-help gurus. My usually impeccable magical control was suffering under the weight of stress. Simple tasks, like summoning a cup of tea, resulted in minor kitchen disasters.

Attempts at discreetly vanishing resulted in a series of spectacularly public reappearances, always accompanied by flashing cameras and the exclamations of breathless onlookers.

My normally calm, controlled demeanor – or what passed for calm in my perpetually grumpy state – had completely disintegrated. The constant pressure of the media, the relentless barrage of questions, and the endless selfies had pushed me to the brink. I felt like a particularly irritable hamster trapped in a giant, glittery exercise wheel.

The worst part? It wasn't even the fame that bothered me most. It was the sheer disruption to my carefully planned retirement. I'd envisioned a peaceful existence, perhaps in a quiet, secluded dimension far removed from the chaotic energy of humans. Instead, my meticulously crafted interdimensional travel coordinates were now plastered across the internet, along with images of my grumpy face, that darned fez, and the now-infamous soufflé incident.

Finding solitude now felt like trying to find a quiet spot in a crowded stadium during a particularly raucous rock concert.

The constant influx of requests for wishes, naturally, had also increased. The internet, it seemed, was convinced that my magical powers were limitless, fueled by the exaggerated portrayal of my abilities on the reality show. People were asking for everything from winning lottery numbers to world peace, apparently believing that a grumpy genie with a malfunctioning magic wand could handle both with equal ease. I had considered filing for a restraining order, but even that would only generate more unwanted attention.

Desperate for some semblance of control, I decided to take a drastic step. I drafted a press release, my fingers flying across the borrowed keyboard. The statement, concise and to the point, was laced with my trademark grumpy wit. "To my valued fans (and those who mistakenly believe I am a source of limitless wishes)," it began. "I am announcing my immediate and permanent retirement. I've had enough of the soufflés, the glitter, the paparazzi, and the endless requests for world peace (which, let me tell you, is not as easy as it sounds). So, I bid farewell. Or should I say, 'Go away and leave me alone.' With that, I shall vanish. Again. If you succeed in finding me, please have a decent cup of tea ready."

I released the statement to the world, with a final, self-satisfied sigh. It hit the internet like a magical meteor, generating an immediate frenzy of speculation and discussion. The next day, I was gone. Not to another dimension, not yet, but to a small, forgotten island. I'd bought the island online with some slightly misdirected magic, and it certainly had a more relaxed vibe than the previous few days had offered. No internet, no paparazzi, and only a few overly friendly crabs. It wasn't exactly the quiet interdimensional retirement I had envisioned, but it was a substantial improvement over viral fame. For now, at least, the Hairy Genie was hiding. The only question was for how long until my next poorly-timed magical mishap made headlines again. And the subsequent media frenzy began once more. I sighed. The life of a genie, even a mildly grumpy one, was never dull.

Unwanted Attention

The peace of my self-imposed exile on Crab Island – a surprisingly accurate name, I might add – was shattered not by a rogue wave or a particularly aggressive crustacean, but by a barrage of emails. My borrowed smartphone, usually dormant beneath a pile of seashells, buzzed incessantly, its screen illuminating the twilight with the garish glow of a thousand unread messages. It appeared my carefully crafted anonymity, achieved by a combination of island-hopping magic and a strategically placed coconut grove, had failed spectacularly.

The emails, a chaotic blend of fan mail, interview requests, and increasingly bizarre conspiracy theories, were overwhelming. One particularly enthusiastic fan suggested we start a genie-themed artisanal soap business, complete with miniature lamp-shaped packaging. Another claimed I was the reincarnation of their pet hamster, a fluffy creature I had never met but somehow felt obligated to apologize to posthumously.

The interview requests were even more bewildering. A representative from "Genie Gossip," a magazine I'd never heard of but somehow suspected involved far too much glitter, wanted an exclusive on my "top five favorite wish-granting moments." A rather aggressively cheerful voice mail message from a daytime talk show host promised a "life-changing opportunity" that sounded suspiciously like public humiliation. Another email, this one more formal, was from a scholarly journal requesting a peer-reviewed paper on the socio-economic implications of reality TV's portrayal of genies. I contemplated using my magic to permanently erase this email from existence, but the sheer absurdity of the situation kept me momentarily enthralled.

My attempts to maintain my cover of a reclusive crab-hermit were, to put it mildly, disastrous. A team from "Extreme Island Getaways," a reality TV show that seemed to specialize in capturing mildly grumpy genies in their natural habitat, managed to find me. Their arrival was heralded by the frantic buzzing of a drone and a rather annoyingly upbeat chant that rhymed "Azrael" with "flaky snail." I had briefly considered hiding behind a particularly large rock, but the sheer indignity of it all made me want to embrace the chaos and possibly teach them a valuable lesson about respecting a genie's downtime.

Escaping their attempts at filming proved more challenging than I'd initially anticipated. My magic, already hampered by stress and a lingering aversion to reality TV, malfunctioned spectacularly. An attempt to conjure a dense fog resulted in a flock of particularly flamboyant parrots that seemed determined to steal my sunglasses.

My plan to teleport myself to a more secluded part of the island ended with me accidentally swapping places with a rather disgruntled seagull, a fact that I quickly realized was far less glamorous than it initially seemed.

Then there was the mail. Mountains of it. Postcards, letters, care packages filled with questionable snacks and bizarre gifts. One contained a handmade knitted genie-sized vest. Another was an unsolicited screenplay for a biopic entitled "The Hairy Genie's Excellent Adventure," which, I must admit, sounded marginally less dreadful than the reality TV show. My attempt to utilize my magic to send it all back resulted in a rather impressive display of spontaneous combustion – involving only the envelopes, thankfully.

Adding to my stress, the internet, even on this remote island, hadn't completely forgotten me. My slightly blurry island paradise pictures surfaced on various social media platforms, my hastily constructed coconut grove acting as a less than ideal disguise. There were endless speculation about my location, cryptic clues that were only slightly more ridiculous than the actual location. My attempts to post vaguely threatening messages were thwarted by well-meaning but clearly very misguided fans, who seemed to interpret my words as encouragement.

One particularly persistent journalist, a woman with a determined glint in her eye and a camera that never seemed to leave her grasp, tracked me down. She was a whirlwind of questions – mostly about my favourite brand of tea (Earl Grey, with a precise amount of milk and sugar, thank you very much) and whether the rumours about my involvement in a clandestine gnome uprising were true (categorically untrue, but the gnomes were surprisingly good at blackmail). I eventually persuaded her to write a story about the importance of respecting a genie's personal space, a subject she seemed genuinely interested in after being chased across a beach by an army of particularly aggressive hermit crabs.

The experience was incredibly stressful, I must confess. My magic was increasingly erratic, my usually mild grumpiness escalating to full-blown genie-rage. I found myself accidentally turning a flock of seagulls into miniature, rather grumpy-looking gnomes, a mistake I sincerely regretted immediately after its occurrence. The gnomes, ironically, turned out to be quite helpful in repelling further unwanted attention, however, their methods were rather questionable and required a great deal of apology afterward.

This particular situation forced me to question my life choices. Had I perhaps chosen the wrong career path? Would a peaceful life tending a flower shop be more fulfilling? Or perhaps a career in artisanal soap-making, a business venture that I found myself strangely drawn to, regardless of the initial absurdity?

But then, a strange thing happened. Amidst the chaos and the unsolicited gnome army, a small, handwritten letter arrived. No cameras, no flashing lights, just a simple note from a young girl who had seen my reality TV appearance. She wrote about how my grumpiness had made her laugh, and how the whole situation had made her think about the importance of kindness and respecting other people's boundaries. It was a simple letter, but it was sincere. And for the first time in days, it made me smile. Maybe the whole reality TV ordeal hadn't been completely disastrous after all.

Perhaps, amidst the chaos, I had unintentionally made a small, positive impact on the world. Perhaps, in time, the unwanted attention will simply fade. Until then, however, I felt a great deal of inspiration, and I began considering writing a book. Perhaps a children's book?

Dealing with Fame

The coconut grove offered surprisingly little solace from the digital deluge. My carefully constructed island paradise, once a haven of peace and quiet (and surprisingly good crab cakes), had become a virtual tourist trap. My face, usually reserved for expressing mild annoyance at incompetent wish-makers, now adorned countless internet memes. "Grumpy Genie Gets Grilled," read one particularly inventive headline, accompanied by a still image of me attempting (and failing) to extinguish a rogue firework with a damp tea towel. Another showed me wrestling a particularly stubborn flamingo – a distinctly un-magical moment – with the caption, "Genie vs. Nature: Round 1 Goes to the Flamingo."

The emails continued. Thousands of them. Requests for autographed teacups (the very one I'd been trapped in, no less).

Marriage proposals (from surprisingly many species). And an alarming number of inquiries about my skincare routine.

Apparently, my perpetually grumpy expression had somehow been deemed "agelessly handsome." The irony was not lost on me.

My attempts at maintaining my newfound "celebrity" status were...less than stellar. I'd tried to embrace the whole internet fame thing, you know, to keep the public appeased. I'd even created a Twitter account (under the handle @GrumpyGenie4Real, naturally) but my attempts at witty tweets were met with deafening silence, except for one particularly enthusiastic fan who kept asking if I could grant him the ability to fly like a flamingo. Apparently, that flamingo incident had a lasting impact.

The interviews were even worse. A morning talk show host, brimming with an unnerving cheerfulness, interrogated me about my "unique perspective on life," while simultaneously attempting to force-feed me a kale smoothie. The taste, I can assure you, was not enhanced by the host's relentless enthusiasm. A late-night talk show host, a man who clearly hadn't slept in decades, tried to convince me to participate in a genie-themed rap battle. I declined. Sharply.

The selfie requests were particularly maddening. Everywhere I went, I was accosted by eager fans, smartphones held aloft, eager to capture a picture with the "internet's grumpiest genie." I began to feel like a particularly hairy zoo animal, constantly being photographed against my will. I tried to explain that I wasn't a fluffy, cuddly mascot; I was a genie, albeit a somewhat malfunctioning one, who preferred solitude to relentless self-promotion. They didn't seem to understand. Or perhaps they did, and the sheer absurdity of my situation amused them. Either way, the selfie requests continued, unabated.

Then came the merchandise. "Grumpy Genie" mugs. "Grumpy Genie" t-shirts. "Grumpy Genie" plushies, that unsettlingly replicated my perpetually furrowed brow. A line of "Grumpy Genie"energy drinks was in development, apparently. The idea of my likeness gracing a caffeinated beverage filled me with a level of dread I hadn't experienced since being trapped in that cursed teacup.

One particularly enterprising company was marketing a line of "Grumpy Genie" stress balls, meticulously crafted to replicate my facial features and general aura of simmering dissatisfaction. I received several boxes of these unsettlingly accurate representations of my current state of being. My initial reaction was one of horror, but it soon morphed into reluctant fascination. I even started using one as a paperweight, finding a strange comfort in the ironic practicality.

The peak of my internet infamy arrived with the release of a documentary about my reality TV debacle. "Genie-uine Chaos,"they'd called it. Clever, I'll give them that. The film chronicled my misadventures with the reality TV crew, focusing heavily on the flamingo incident and my less-than-graceful attempts to escape from a particularly overzealous cameraman. The ending credits featured footage of the various "Grumpy Genie" merchandise items, set to an upbeat, ironically jaunty tune. I nearly choked on a particularly bland cracker upon viewing it.

The documentary was a smash hit, catapulting my "fame" to previously unimaginable heights. My island retreat was overrun by paparazzi, who seemed to be emerging from the sea itself. The crab cakes were ruined, the peace was shattered, and the coconut grove now sported a rather unwelcome collection of paparazzi drones.

I tried various methods to regain my anonymity. I dyed my beard bright purple (it clashed horribly with my complexion). I attempted to blend in with a flock of particularly grumpy-looking seagulls (they weren't impressed). I even considered changing my name."Bartholomew Bumblebrook" had a certain ring to it. But nothing worked. The internet had a hold on me, and it wasn't about to let go.

One day, amidst the chaos, a small package arrived. No cameras, no flashing lights, just a plain brown box. Inside, nestled amongst packing peanuts, was a single, perfectly baked, gluten-free, sugar-free, dairy-free, nut-free, soy-free, and egg-free crab cake. A handwritten note accompanied it: "Thought you might need this. A fan who appreciates good crab cakes and understands the value of a quiet life."

It wasn't a glamorous solution, but it was a start. A small, delicious, and utterly anonymous crumb of comfort in the overwhelming whirlwind of my newfound "fame." Maybe, just maybe, I could navigate this bizarre reality. Perhaps, even, I could learn to appreciate the occasional, well-baked crab cake. After all, even a grumpy genie deserves a treat now and again. And maybe, just maybe, I'd write that children's book after all. It could be about a grumpy genie who learns to appreciate the quiet moments, even amidst the chaos. Or maybe about a flamingo who dreams of becoming a rap star. The possibilities, as they say, were endless. And I suddenly felt... a tiny spark of something resembling hope.

The Price of Fame

The escape plan, meticulously crafted over several lukewarm crab cakes and a surprisingly insightful documentary about the mating rituals of pygmy marmosets (who, it turned out, were far more organized than most humans), was, in retrospect, hopelessly naive. I'd envisioned a quiet, unassuming departure, perhaps a discreet flitting away to a dimension where the only requests involved the precise brewing temperature for Earl Grey tea. Instead, my attempt at retirement resembled the chaotic finale of a particularly low-budget action movie.

My chosen mode of transportation – a slightly battered, second-hand hover-scooter I'd acquired from a suspiciously friendly gnome– was no match for the paparazzi horde. They swarmed me like particularly aggressive wasps, their cameras flashing with the intensity of a thousand tiny suns. I tried invisibility, a spell I'd always found rather unreliable (it often resulted in me being partially invisible, leaving me looking like a bizarre, shimmering half-genie). It didn't work. Apparently, in the age of high-definition cameras and relentless social media, even partial invisibility was no deterrent to a pack of fame-hungry photographers.

One particularly intrepid reporter, a young woman with a shockingly bright pink bob and an even brighter smile, managed to snag an interview mid-air. "So, Azrael," she chirped, her voice barely audible above the roar of the hover-scooter's engine, "rumors are flying! Are you really retiring? Is the self-help guru story true? Are you a fan of flamingo wrestling? And most importantly, what's your secret to that ridiculously fabulous beard?"

My attempts at dignified silence were met with a barrage of increasingly impertinent questions. I considered using a silencing spell, but then realized that doing so would likely make me the subject of even more intense speculation. "The beard," I muttered, grabbing at a stray strand that had decided to embark on its own independent journey, "is entirely natural. And please, maintain some distance. This hover-scooter is not exactly known for its advanced safety features."

The chase continued, weaving through bustling city streets, narrowly avoiding a collision with a bewildered flock of pigeons and a surprisingly agile hot dog vendor. It felt like a scene from a slapstick comedy, albeit one I had no desire to star in. Every attempt to lose them only seemed to attract more attention. News helicopters buzzed overhead, their cameras capturing my every awkward maneuver. My retirement was officially trending.

I even tried blending in with a group of mime artists. It was as disastrous as it sounds. Turns out, a grumpy genie in mid-mime is significantly more unsettling than a grumpy genie on a hover-scooter. One particularly imaginative onlooker posted a photo online with the caption: "Is that a genie...or an extra-terrestrial mime who's just had a very bad day?" The comment section erupted with imaginative theories, from interdimensional travel to an elaborate marketing campaign for a new brand of beard oil.

Clearly, my ability to blend into my surroundings had become inversely proportional to my fame.

The culmination of this absurd chase arrived unexpectedly – at the annual convention for professional flamingo wranglers. Apparently, there was such a thing. And, apparently, my now-infamous flamingo wrestling photo had made me an honorary guest.

The convention hall was a cacophony of squawking birds, enthusiastic trainers, and a disturbingly large supply of flamingo-themed merchandise. I found myself seated on a plush flamingo-shaped cushion, next to a woman who claimed to have trained her prize-winning flamingo, Carlos, to perform complex ballet moves (Carlos, in protest, promptly pecked her on the nose). The interview requests continued relentlessly. Each question, a tiny peck at my rapidly dwindling patience. How *dare* they subject me to yet another flamingo-related inquiry? I was a genie, for crying out loud, not an avian acrobat!

The reality of my "fame" hit me with the force of a particularly aggressive flamingo wing. It wasn't just about the constant intrusion; it was the sheer absurdity of it all. My retirement had become a spectacle, my escape a chase. The whole situation was a surreal tapestry woven with threads of mistaken identity, accidental fame, and a significant amount of flamingo-related stress. Perhaps the quiet life I'd envisioned was nothing but a distant mirage.

Later that night, after successfully evading another group of persistent paparazzi (using a decoy comprised of a rather convincing inflatable genie and a strategically placed smoke bomb), I found myself sitting alone, staring at the night sky. The stars, usually a source of quiet contemplation, now felt like the unblinking eyes of a global audience. My retirement seemed a distant dream now.

The next morning, I received an offer I couldn't refuse. Or rather, an offer I couldn't ignore. A prominent reality TV network wanted me for a spin-off show: "Grumpy Genie Goes Global." The concept, they explained, involved me traveling the world, helping people with their wishes, and wrestling more flamingos (apparently, that part was very popular). They offered a hefty sum, a contract that included a generous clause on the provision of high-quality crab cakes, and a team dedicated to helping me evade paparazzi (a surprisingly large team).

The absurdity of the situation was almost overwhelming. A grumpy genie, unwilling participant in his own fame, turned into a reality TV star? I considered rejecting the offer, retreating to a secluded island where crab cakes were plentiful, and flamingos were not. But the thought of that hefty sum, coupled with an endless supply of high-quality crab cakes, was an irresistible lure. Besides, maybe I could use this platform to educate people about the finer points of genie etiquette and the importance of reading clause 3b in any wish-granting contract.

The road to retirement was going to be a lot longer and more circuitous than I'd anticipated. But perhaps, just perhaps, with a dash of crab cake-fueled optimism, even a grumpy genie could navigate the treacherous waters of fame and, at some point far in the future, actually attain a peaceful, quiet retirement. The thought itself, was almost enough to make me smile - almost. Until, of course, another paparazzi chase began. The flamingo wrestling championships were next week, and apparently, I was the star attraction. I groaned. Some days, being a genie felt less like magic, and more like a very elaborate, very public, and very feathered form of self-punishment.

A Very Public Retirement

The flamingo wrestling championships loomed, a monstrous pink cloud on the horizon of my already disastrous week. Escaping the relentless paparazzi felt less like a strategic retreat and more like a desperate game of hide-and-seek with a pack of particularly persistent badgers. Each flash of their cameras felt like a tiny, infuriating jab of magical energy draining from me. My powers, already depleted from a week of incompetent wish-granting and reality TV shenanigans, were dwindling faster than my dwindling supply of Earl Grey tea.

I needed a solution, and quickly. Running away, as appealing as it initially sounded, wasn't proving very effective. I needed a grand, sweeping gesture, something to make the media, and more importantly, myself, understand that this whole genie-thing wasn't exactly my ideal life plan. An idea, as brilliant as it was improbable, began to form in my mind: a public retirement.

Yes, a very public retirement. I would not simply fade away. I would announce my departure with the flamboyant theatricality only a chronically exasperated genie could muster. I envisioned myself on a stage, bathed in the shimmering light of a thousand flashbulbs, a microphone clutched in my hand, delivering a farewell address that would resonate for centuries – or at least, until the next celebrity scandal broke.

First, I needed a press release. I summoned a quill (slightly bent, but functional) and a scroll of particularly high-quality parchment (it had felt rather rude to use something less than premium quality when making such a momentous announcement). The process of crafting my announcement proved to be surprisingly difficult. Keeping my message concise, yet impactful, while still allowing for the necessary level of grumpy pronouncements, was challenging.

My initial drafts ranged from passive-aggressive to outright belligerent. One draft ended with a darkly humorous threat to unleash a swarm of particularly aggressive squirrels on anyone who dared to continue summoning me. I eventually settled on a more measured approach, though a hint of my simmering irritation still managed to seep through.

The press release, once finalized, was as follows:

"FOR IMMEDIATE RELEASE

GENIE AZRAEL ANNOUNCES RETIREMENT

After centuries of providing wishes (mostly underwhelming ones, might I add), I, Azrael, am announcing my official retirement from the genie business. Effective immediately, I will be unavailable for any further wish-granting activities. This decision, while difficult, is entirely necessary. The sheer incompetence displayed by the vast majority of humans has proven to be more exhausting than battling a hydra with a rusty spork.

Furthermore, the constant barrage of paparazzi, reality TV crews, and self-help gurus has rendered my once-impressive magical capabilities significantly diminished. My powers, once capable of summoning elephants from thin air, are now struggling to conjure a decent cup of tea. The decline has been alarmingly rapid and, frankly, quite insulting to my centuries of experience.

I wish (pun intended, and regretfully so) all future wish-granting hopefuls the best of luck. You will need it. And please, for the love of all that is magically sane, read the fine print. Clause 3b will be the death of you.

Sincerely (and with a monumental sigh),

Azrael"

With the press release sent, I braced myself for the inevitable media frenzy. And it was, as expected, epic.

The news channels went wild. Headline screamed, "GENIE QUITS! IS IT THE STRAW THAT BROKE THE CAMEL'S BACK?" and "AZRAEL: THE GRUMPIEST GENIE EVER – CALLS IT QUITS!" Talk shows were consumed with discussions about my retirement, and various experts – including a surprisingly confident astrologer who claimed my retirement was aligned with a rare planetary conjunction – weighed in on the matter.

My doorbell rang incessantly. Reporters, photographers, and even a couple of enthusiastic cosplayers dressed as particularly flamboyant djinn, descended upon my humble abode. I spent the afternoon fielding questions, delivering gruff responses, and dodging microphones with the agility of a caffeinated squirrel. One particularly tenacious reporter followed me into my bathroom, asking about my skincare routine. Another tried to interview me while I was attempting to make myself a cup of (still stubbornly difficult to conjure) tea.

The climax of the media circus came during a live television interview. I was perched on a rather uncomfortable velvet chair, facing a panel of three exceptionally enthusiastic hosts. They peppered me with questions, ranging from the mundane ("What's your favorite type of tea?") to the strangely philosophical ("Does immortality feel like a blessing or a curse?"). My answers were suitably blunt and often laced with sardonic wit.

“Immortality? It's like having a very, very long to-do list that never quite gets completed," I grumbled, sipping my lukewarm tea. "And the to-do list mainly consists of dealing with the incredibly poor decision-making skills of humanity.”

The interview was a triumph of controlled exasperation. I managed to convey my message – a firm "goodbye" to the world of wish-granting – while simultaneously entertaining the audience with my signature blend of grumpy charm and magically-fueled sarcasm.

The show's producers were ecstatic. They claimed it was the highest-rated interview they'd had all year.

My retirement, initially conceived as a quiet escape, had transformed into a spectacle of epic proportions. It was exhausting, yes, but in a strange, oddly satisfying way. After the last interview, after the last flashbulb had faded, after the last reporter had shuffled out of my house, I finally felt a sense of peace. The peace that comes from knowing you've publicly and spectacularly thrown in the towel. Now, about that Earl Grey... Maybe, just maybe, in retirement, I could finally master its perfect brewing temperature. And perhaps, perhaps, I might even smile. Almost.

The Interdimensional Escape

The shimmering portal, painstakingly constructed from repurposed teacup shards and a surprisingly potent blend of chamomile tea and disillusionment, flickered ominously. Azrael, clutching a battered travel guide titled "Interdimensional Retirement Destinations: A Genie's Guide to Tranquility (Mostly)," adjusted his fez, a gesture that did little to alleviate his mounting anxiety. Retirement. The very word hummed with the promise of blissful solitude, a realm devoid of reality TV crews, philosophical pigeons, and self-help gurus with an alarmingly positive outlook.

He'd spent centuries – well, more like millennia, give or take a few centuries of bureaucratic snafus with the Genie Union – granting wishes. Most of them had involved lost socks, minor lottery wins, and the inexplicable desire for a singing hamster. The sheer monotony had chipped away at his already grumpy disposition, leaving him with the magical equivalent of a chronic case of the Mondays.

But today, today was different. Today, Azrael was attempting the ultimate wish – a wish for escape.

He'd meticulously calculated the coordinates, consulted ancient scrolls (mostly coffee-stained and riddled with cryptic annotations), and even sacrificed a perfectly good fig newton to the capricious whims of interdimensional travel. The portal shimmered again, a sickly green glow radiating a palpable sense of impending doom.

"Right then," he muttered, adjusting the dial on his (frankly outdated) interdimensional travel device – a contraption cobbled together from spare parts scavenged from various forgotten dimensions. It looked suspiciously like a toaster oven with wires sprouting from every conceivable angle. "Let's get this over with."He took a deep breath, reminding himself of his mantra: "Grumpy, yes, but not incompetent (mostly)."

With a dramatic flourish (which, admittedly, was more of a twitch than a flourish), he stepped into the portal. A kaleidoscope of swirling colors assaulted his senses, a chaotic ballet of light and sound that left him feeling rather nauseous. He braced himself for a smooth, effortless transition to a serene paradise, somewhere possibly filled with endless supplies of lukewarm tea and the complete absence of demanding humans.

Then, the device sputtered.

The portal, instead of transporting him to a peaceful haven, deposited him with a disconcerting *thump* into... a teacup.

Not just any teacup. A *sentient* teacup.

This teacup, a delicate porcelain creation adorned with a rather smug-looking cherub, regarded him with a distinctly condescending stare. "Well, well," the teacup chirped, its voice surprisingly deep for something so small, "another one. Are you here for the philosophical debate? We're discussing the merits of Earl Grey versus Darjeeling, and the implications for the very fabric of reality."

Azrael blinked. This was not the serene retirement he'd envisioned.

He was, once again, trapped. But this time, it wasn't a clueless magician or a forgetful librarian; it was a judgmental teacup. The irony, he mused, was almost as bitter as the chamomile tea he'd been forced to drink earlier.

"Philosophical debate?" he grumbled, dusting himself off. He was, after all, still a genie, even if a thoroughly disgruntled one. "I'm here for retirement, not a seminar on tea-based metaphysics."

The teacup scoffed, a delicate, yet somehow menacing sound. "Retirement? Preposterous! In this dimension, we have rigorous schedules. Afternoon tea is promptly at 3:17, followed by the mandatory existential crisis discussion. Then, there's the biscuit-dunking protocol... it's rather complex."

The teacup continued its tirade, detailing the intricacies of teacup society, a rigid hierarchy governed by the precise angle of the handle and the subtly nuanced variations in porcelain glaze. Azrael, meanwhile, was finding himself increasingly overwhelmed. The sheer level of detail, the obsession with tea-related etiquette – it was all far too much. He was used to dealing with the irrationality of humans, but these sentient teacups were in a league of their own.

Days blurred into weeks. Azrael found himself participating in endless tea parties, engaging in debates about the relative merits of different types of milk (oat, almond, soy – the sheer audacity!), and even mastering the art of the perfect biscuit dunk. He learned to navigate the treacherous social landscape of teacup society,
avoiding the notoriously sharp-tongued bone china elite and the perpetually grumpy demitasse crowd.

His escape attempts were thwarted by an intricate system of magically-reinforced tea cosies and impossibly small, yet incredibly strong, tea strainers. He'd tried using his magic, naturally, but his attempts to teleport himself back to his own dimension resulted only in the accidental summoning of a flock of miniature, extremely opinionated squirrels who insisted on discussing the aesthetics of teacup handles.

In time, however, a strange thing began to happen. The relentless rhythm of tea parties, debates, and biscuit dunking started to become... less irritating. The constant chatter, once a source of immense annoyance, began to take on a peculiar comfort. Azrael, to his surprise, even found himself enjoying a particularly well-brewed Earl Grey.

He discovered a sense of peace in the predictability of it all, a stark contrast to the chaotic unpredictability of the human world. He'd expected retirement to be a quiet escape, but this... this was different. It was a strangely satisfying chaos, a structured absurdity that somehow fit.

One afternoon, during a heated debate about the ideal temperature for chamomile tea, Azrael found himself surprisingly contributing to the discussion. He even offered a compelling argument regarding the impact of altitude on brewing techniques. He sighed. It seemed that retirement, in its own peculiar way, had found him. Even if that retirement involved an endless supply of meticulously brewed tea and the constant threat of a well-aimed biscuit dunk. He took a sip of tea. "At least it's warm," he grumbled, with a hint of something close to contentment in his voice. The teacup across from him shuddered slightly. The debate was on again.

Unexpected Detour

The portal, a shimmering vortex of chamomile-infused chaos, spat Azrael out not onto a serene, retirement-ready planet, but into... a teacup. Not just any teacup, mind you. This was a teacup of considerable girth, adorned with a rather fetching floral pattern, and possessing, to Azrael's utter astonishment, a surprisingly high-pitched voice.

"Well, hello there, you magnificent, slightly disheveled... thing!" the teacup chirped, its handle jiggling excitedly. "Welcome to Teacuptopia!"

Azrael, still reeling from the unexpected spatial displacement, blinked. Teacuptopia? He'd envisioned a quiet cottage by a babbling brook, perhaps a hammock strung between two ancient, philosophical oak trees. Not a dimension populated entirely by sentient teacups. His retirement guide had clearly omitted this particular detail. Clause 3b, perhaps? He'd always suspected clause 3b was the root of all his genie-related problems.

"I... I believe there's been a slight... misunderstanding," Azrael stammered, attempting to adjust his fez for the tenth time in as many minutes. The fez, sadly, was feeling rather crushed from its journey through the portal. "I was aiming for... well, somewhere less... cup-centric."

"Oh, nonsense!" the large floral teacup, who introduced himself as Reginald, declared. "Teacuptopia is marvelous! We have exquisite tea blends, lively debates on the merits of bone china versus porcelain, and the most thrilling saucer-sliding competitions you ever did see."

Reginald proceeded to give Azrael a whirlwind tour of Teacuptopia. It was, admittedly, rather charming in its own peculiar way. The city was built into the side of a colossal teapot, complete with tiny, perfectly formed teacup houses, each with its own miniature garden meticulously crafted from sugar cubes and dried herbs. Teacup citizens, ranging in size and style from delicate demitasses to sturdy mugs, bustled about, engaged in various activities. Some were engaged in passionate arguments about the optimal brewing temperature for Earl Grey, others were meticulously polishing their handles, while a few were participating in a surprisingly competitive game of "Handle-to-Handle Combat," which involved surprisingly aggressive maneuvering of their handles.

Azrael, however, was still grappling with the fact that he'd inadvertently traded his impending retirement for a life amongst sentient teacups. He tried to discreetly consult his "Interdimensional Retirement Destinations" guide, but the book had suffered some minor... structural damage during the portal transition. Several pages were now stuck together, forming a rather unappetizing paste of chamomile tea and questionable travel advice.

"So," Reginald chirped, interrupting Azrael's silent lament, "what brings a... uh... *genie* to our humble abode?"

Azrael sighed. Explaining the intricacies of accidental interdimensional travel to a sentient teacup was proving more challenging than he'd anticipated. He opted for a simplified version.

"Let's just say I was looking for a quiet place to... retire. Away from... humans."

Reginald tilted his handle thoughtfully. "Humans, eh? We've heard tales. Apparently, they're rather clumsy and prone to... well, breaking things. We're quite fond of our integrity, you see."

Azrael couldn't help but chuckle. At least the teacups possessed a certain self-awareness. The humans he'd encountered, on the other hand... well, let's just say their self-awareness was a bit... selective.

Over the next few days, Azrael found himself surprisingly adapting to life in Teacuptopia. He discovered a hidden talent for miniature teacup gardening, achieving a surprisingly bountiful harvest of sugar cube carrots. He even participated in a saucer-sliding competition, surprisingly placing third, though he suspected the judges were swayed by his dazzling fez. The competition, he learned, was judged primarily on the "dazzle factor" and the "general air of mystique." He excelled in both.

He also found himself drawn into the seemingly endless debates about tea. He discovered that his human-acquired knowledge of various brewing techniques actually proved invaluable in the teapot-shaped city. He became a sort of consultant, offering his unique perspective on optimal steeping times, water temperatures, and the subtle art of creating the perfect crema on a frothy cappuccino (a rather unusual tea-based beverage popular among the more adventurous teacups).

One evening, while sipping a particularly potent blend of Darjeeling and chamomile (a local specialty), Azrael overheard a conversation between two teacups concerning a rumor of a way back to his original dimension. It seemed there was a legendary "Teapot Transporter," a mythical device capable of shuttling travelers between dimensions. The catch? It was hidden somewhere within the colossal teapot that formed the city. A legendary quest, then, seemingly tailored for a mildly grumpy genie with a penchant for solving problems through rather unusual means.

Azrael, despite his initial reluctance, found a strange sense of purpose, a glimmer of excitement in his previously retirement-weary eyes. Perhaps retirement wasn't quite what he had initially planned, but the adventure, the camaraderie, and the surprisingly high-quality tea had its own peculiar charm. He wasn't sure what to expect, but as Reginald offered him another cup of the Darjeeling-chamomile blend, a new thought crept into his mind: Retirement, maybe, could wait. First, he needed to find a legendary teapot transporter. And maybe, just maybe, learn to slide a saucer with more grace. The competitive spirit, it seemed, was slowly awakening within him. The quest for the Teapot Transporter began the following morning, accompanied by a rather enthusiastic chorus of cheering teacups and a somewhat hesitant Reginald, worried about the potential for handle-related damage. After all, this wasn't just any old quest. This was a quest involving a grumpy genie, a city made of teacups, and an absolutely vital supply of exceptional tea. And that, Azrael knew, was anything but ordinary. His retirement, it seemed, would have to wait. For now, he was far too busy finding the Teapot Transporter to even think about it. And besides, the view from the top of the giant teapot was quite breathtaking.

A New Set of Problems

The sun, a hazy orange orb through the swirling steam of a thousand miniature teacups, cast long shadows across the city of Cerámica. Azrael, perched precariously on the rim of a particularly ornate floral teacup, sighed. Retirement, it seemed, was proving more elusive than a particularly elusive crumb in a poorly swept pantry. The sentient teacups, it turned out, were even more demanding than the humans he'd left behind.

His initial days in Cerámica had been… interesting. A charming, if slightly chaotic, introduction to a society where the proper brewing temperature of Darjeeling was a matter of life and death, and the etiquette for miniature genie interactions was far more complex than any human social convention he'd encountered. Reginald, the teacup who'd initially rescued him from the portal, had become a surprisingly loyal companion, though his constant need to discuss the merits of porcelain versus ceramic was wearing thin.

"Azrael, my dear fellow," Reginald chirped, his voice a high-pitched tinkle, "have you considered the existential implications of a chipped handle? It speaks to the fragility of existence, wouldn't you agree?"

Azrael rubbed his temples, wishing, not for the first time, for the simple, if occasionally infuriating, requests of humans. "Reginald, I'm trying to find a teapot transporter. The existential implications of a chipped handle can wait until after I've successfully relocated myself to a dimension with less… teacup-related philosophical debates."

The problem, as Azrael soon discovered, wasn't just the philosophical bent of the Cerámica residents. They were also exceptionally demanding regarding their tea. The finest leaves, brewed at precisely the right temperature, served in the most aesthetically pleasing cups – these were non-negotiable requirements. Azrael, whose magical abilities were, to put it mildly, unreliable, frequently found himself struggling to conjure the perfect cuppa. His attempts often resulted in lukewarm, oddly bitter concoctions that left the teacups muttering darkly about the decline of genie-provided hospitality.

"This is an outrage!" shrieked a particularly flamboyant teacup with a gilded handle. "This tea lacks the necessary zest! It's as if a goblin brewed it with his muddy boots!"

Azrael, battling a sudden surge of self-doubt and a profound craving for a decent cup of coffee (which, sadly, was not available in Cerámica), sighed again. This wasn't the peaceful retirement he'd envisioned. This was more like an endless tea party from hell, hosted by a chorus of extremely opinionated china.

Their demands extended beyond tea. They wanted stories, poems, even elaborate theatrical performances. Azrael, who considered his storytelling abilities to be mildly adequate at best, found himself reluctantly reciting limericks, improvising Shakespearean sonnets (with surprisingly disastrous results), and even attempting a dramatic reading of the teacup city's by-laws. The latter nearly resulted in a riot.

"He mispronounced 'porcelain'!" a small, chipped teacup declared, his voice trembling with indignation. "The performance was utterly dreadful! We demand a refund of our emotional energy!"

Finding the legendary teapot transporter seemed increasingly unlikely, overshadowed by the daily struggle to meet the ever-growing demands of his tiny, highly critical audience. Azrael contemplated making a run for it, but the city walls were impossibly high, and, more importantly, covered in a particularly thorny variety of tea-scented rose bushes. Escape seemed even less appealing than facing another round of philosophical debates about the nature of being.

One particularly frustrating afternoon, while attempting to conjure a particularly elusive variety of Himalayan black tea (the teacups were nothing if not pretentious), Azrael stumbled upon a hidden library tucked away in a shadowy corner of the city. It wasn't filled with dusty tomes, but with meticulously organized tea leaves, each variety carefully labelled and catalogued. Azrael, feeling the weight of his numerous failures, decided to take a break from his duties and delve into the library. Perhaps some research could help him in his quest. Maybe this library held some clue to the location of the legendary teapot transporter, a way out of this miniature hell of high-strung teacups and their endless demands.

But the library, it turned out, was guarded by a tiny, fiercely protective teapot named Bartholomew, who looked like a miniature, disgruntled volcano. He regarded Azrael with suspicion, his spout quivering slightly. "Intruders!" he squeaked, his voice surprisingly deep for his size. "Begone, you clumsy genie, before I unleash the full force of my... well, my terrible temper!"

Bartholomew's temper, it turned out, involved throwing loose tea leaves with alarming accuracy. Azrael, dodging the projectile caffeinated projectiles, realized that finding the teapot transporter was going to require more than just a little magic. It was going to require diplomacy, cunning, and possibly a very large supply of the finest Earl Grey. He sighed again, accepting the reality that his retirement was going to take a little longer than he'd initially hoped.

The next few days were a whirlwind of carefully brewed teas, hastily improvised poetry readings, and delicate negotiations with the inhabitants of Cerámica. Azrael, surprisingly, began to find a strange rhythm to this bizarre existence. He learned to anticipate the teacups' needs, to discern their moods from the subtle shifts in their porcelain expressions. He even started to enjoy the intellectual sparring, the high-stakes arguments about the optimal brewing time for Darjeeling, the fierce debates over the proper placement of sugar cubes. He found himself defending his poetry more vehemently than he ever defended his magical abilities back in the human realm.

He found a strange camaraderie with Reginald, a grudging respect for Bartholomew, and even a begrudging fondness for the demanding teacups that dominated his days. Retirement, he realized, wasn't about escaping the world; it was about finding a place where he could be, perhaps imperfectly, at peace. And perhaps, just perhaps, Cerámica, the city of demanding teacups and never-ending tea parties, was slowly but surely becoming that place. The quest for the teapot transporter continued, of course, but the urgency had lessened. It had become less a desperate escape, and more a pleasant adventure, seasoned with high-quality tea and the surprisingly invigorating company of his eccentric, ceramic friends. Retirement could wait. For now, he had a city of teacups to manage, a reputation as a poet to defend, and a bottomless supply of Darjeeling to brew. And that, he decided, wasn't so bad after all.

Acceptance of Fate

The iridescent shimmer of a particularly plump, porcelain butterfly–one of Reginald's more extravagant creations – caught Azrael's eye. He'd spent the last few days attempting to decipher Reginald's cryptic pronouncements on the nature of truly excellent Earl Grey, a topic Reginald treated with the seriousness usually reserved for matters of state. Reginald, it turned out, wasn't just a teacup; he was a connoisseur, a philosopher, a cermaic Socrates steeped in the fragrant wisdom of a thousand brewed leaves.

Azrael, perched atop a miniature replica of the Eiffel Tower (a rather unstable perch, he admitted), chuckled softly. Retirement, he'd decided, wasn't a place; it was a state of mind. Or perhaps, more accurately, a state of mild, tea-soaked contentment. The frantic escape from the human realm, once a burning desire, had faded into a distant memory, replaced by the surprisingly soothing rhythm of Cerámica's daily tea rituals.

Bartholomew, the ever-practical teacup with a penchant for practical jokes (mostly involving miniature sugar tongs and unsuspecting butterflies), popped his head around a towering stack of Darjeeling tins. "You're awfully quiet today, Azrael," he observed, his voice a surprisingly deep baritone for a teacup of his size.

"Contemplating the universe, Bartholomew," Azrael replied, swirling a tiny cup of his own, the brew a shimmering amber. "Or, more accurately, contemplating the surprisingly philosophical depth of Earl Grey."

Bartholomew grunted. "Philosophical depth? It's tea, Azrael. Drink it, enjoy it, and move on to the next cup. Unless," he added with a mischievous glint, "you've found a way to brew it with actual magic?"

"Tempting," Azrael admitted, "but I believe I'm content with the slightly less explosive approach. Though I do have a half-formed theory involving moonbeams and a pinch of cinnamon…"

The idea, unfortunately, led to a spirited (and rather messy) debate on the merits of moonlight-infused tea, a discussion punctuated by the occasional accidental geyser of bubbling brew and Bartholomew's increasingly frantic attempts to salvage the situation with strategically placed napkins.

Their impromptu tea party was interrupted by the arrival of Penelope, a rather flamboyant teacup with a penchant for dramatic poetry and an alarming habit of tipping over during particularly passionate recitations. She launched into a lengthy ode to the glories of porcelain, her words flowing like a river of liquid eloquence.

Azrael, despite himself, found himself drawn into the poetic rhythm, the words painting vivid images of shimmering teacups under a twilight sky. Retirement, he realized, wasn't about escaping the chaos; it was about finding a way to appreciate the beauty within it, to find the poetry in the everyday. Even in the midst of a chaotic teacup-based society.

The following days unfolded in a pattern of gentle chaos. There were impromptu tea ceremonies with elaborate rituals, philosophical debates on the optimal brewing temperature, and the occasional near-catastrophic mishap involving a rogue sugar cube and a particularly volatile blend of chamomile.

Azrael discovered a hidden talent for tea-leaf fortune-telling, his predictions often oddly accurate despite his reliance on pure guesswork and an impressive amount of caffeine. He even started writing poetry, his verses filled with witty observations about the lives of the teacups, their quirks and their dreams. His poetic voice earned him a level of respect, a surprising amount of fan mail written in tiny, elegant script, and an invitation to read his work at the upcoming Cerámica Ceramic Convention.

His relationship with Reginald blossomed into a surprisingly deep friendship. Azrael learned to appreciate the subtlety of different tea blends and discovered a shared love for obscure historical anecdotes about the history of teapots. He and Bartholomew engaged in philosophical debates on the nature of reality, with Bartholomew usually winning by sheer force of his stubbornness and Azrael by sheer wit. Even Penelope, with her dramatic recitations and tendency towards theatrical outbursts, became a valued companion, her chaotic energy somehow balancing the quiet contemplation of Azrael's own existence.

The search for the teapot transporter continued, of course. It remained a quaint side project, a goal less frantic, more of a whimsical hobby. Azrael found that he had little urge to rush; the quest felt less like an escape and more like a delightful adventure intertwined with the daily routines of his newly adopted ceramic life. The transporter might appear one day, perhaps in the bottom of a particularly large teacup, or maybe hidden within the pages of a dusty tome of tea-related folklore. But the urgency had vanished, replaced by a newfound contentment.

One evening, under the soft glow of a thousand teacup lights, Azrael sat with Reginald, Bartholomew and Penelope, sipping a particularly exquisite blend of jasmine tea. The conversation drifted from the philosophical implications of a chipped teacup to the merits of various types of tea infusers.

"Retirement, it seems," Azrael said, a smile playing on his lips, "is rather different from what I expected."

Bartholomew snorted. "Expected? You expected to retire from *us* ?"

Reginald nodded sagely. "Indeed. We are not easily retired from, Azrael. We are a force to be reckoned with. A force...of...tea."

Penelope, ever dramatic, added, "A force of brewed destiny, a tempest in a teapot, a...a..." She struggled to find the right word, then gave up with a dramatic sigh. "A wonderfully chaotic tea party."

Azrael laughed, a genuine, hearty laugh that resonated in the quiet room. He looked around at his ceramic friends, at the warm glow of the teacups, at the comforting scent of jasmine in the air. He realized that he wasn't just accepting his fate, he was embracing it.

Retirement, he mused, might be just around the corner, hidden somewhere within the infinite possibilities of a never-ending tea party. But for now, he was content, surrounded by unlikely friends, in a world far removed from the human chaos he had once so desperately wanted to escape. The world, it turned out, was a much stranger, and more delightful place, than he had ever imagined. It was a place of vibrant porcelain, endless tea parties, and unexpected friendships. And he wouldn't have it any other way. The tea, after all, was quite excellent. And the company, even more so.

Retirement could wait. For now, there was a city of teacups to manage, a reputation to maintain, and a bottomless supply of Darjeeling to brew. And, in this moment, surrounded by his eccentric ceramic family, he knew he wouldn't trade it for all the wishes in the world. Perhaps clause 3b of the genie contract wasn't so bad after all. Perhaps, just perhaps, he'd finally found his happily ever after, served in a perfectly delightful teacup.

A Grumpy Conclusion

The iridescent shimmer of the porcelain butterfly faded as Azrael adjusted to his new reality – a reality less chaotic than he'd anticipated, yet oddly...tepid. He'd expected a grand, fiery entrance into retirement, perhaps a celestial fanfare, a welcoming committee of retired genies lounging on cloud-like chaise longues. Instead, he found himself nestled amongst a rather large collection of mismatched teacups, a gentle hum of ceramic contentment the only soundtrack to his newfound leisure.

Reginald, bless his tiny, tea-stained heart, had been right. The world beyond the human realm was, indeed, stranger than fiction, but in a surprisingly delightful way. He'd made friends with a chipped teacup named Beatrice who claimed to be a former royal goblet (a rather dubious claim, Azrael suspected, given her propensity for collecting stray sugar granules), and a rather flamboyant espresso cup named Fernando who spent his days practicing operatic arias. Their conversations, though often punctuated by the clinking of ceramic bodies and the occasional tremor from a nearby earthquake (apparently, this dimension had a fondness for seismic activity), were far more entertaining than the endless stream of inept wishes he'd endured in the human world.

The humans, he realized, weren't entirely incompetent. They were simply...flamboyantly incompetent. Their clumsiness, their baffling decisions, their utter disregard for the fine print – it was all part of their endearingly chaotic charm. He'd spent centuries battling their ineptitude, but now, removed from the fray, the absurdity of it all struck him as oddly...comforting. It was like watching a particularly slapstick comedy, a never-ending string of hilarious mishaps, only this time, he was sipping Earl Grey from a perfectly formed porcelain cup and not caught in the middle of the mayhem.

There was a certain perverse satisfaction in observing their struggles from afar. He'd once dreamt of escaping the endless stream of poorly conceived wishes, the constant barrage of unreasonable demands. Now, separated from it all, he found himself missing the very thing he'd so desperately wanted to avoid. It wasn't the wishes themselves he missed, oh no. It was the sheer, unadulterated absurdity of it all. The magician who'd trapped him in a teacup, the librarian who'd unleashed him while searching for a particularly dusty copy of "Muttering Genies for Beginners," the reality TV crew who mistook him for a particularly hairy extra -each encounter was a comedic masterpiece in its own right.

He'd even grown fond of the self-help guru, the incredibly self-assured, impossibly dense man whose self-help seminars seemed to generate more chaos than they solved. The man, whose name Azrael had thankfully forgotten (a mercy, considering the effort it took to pronounce), represented the peak of human absurdity. He was a walking, talking embodiment of flawed logic, a master of self-deception wrapped in a tailored suit and an aura of unshakeable confidence. And yet, Azrael had found himself strangely captivated by his sheer audacity.

Retirement, he realized, wasn't about escaping the human race entirely. It was about finding a new perspective, a new appreciation for the chaos he'd once so desperately wanted to leave behind. It was about finding the humor in the absurdity, the beauty in the unexpected, and the comfort in a perfectly brewed cup of tea, even if the tea itself was slightly lukewarm.

Yes, the tea was a slight problem. It had been lukewarm that morning and remained so throughout the day. This, Azrael was beginning to suspect, was the biggest inconvenience of retirement. In the human world, at least, he had the satisfaction of knowing his discomfort was shared with the general population. Here, in his new ceramic community, the temperature of his tea was entirely his burden to bear. It wasn't a catastrophic problem, not exactly, but it did chip away at the perfection of his retirement.

He sighed, a puff of perfectly harmless, non-magical air. He'd expected the afterlife, or whatever this dimension was supposed to be, to be more...dramatic. More fulfilling. Less...tepid. The porcelain butterfly, still perched on the rim of his teacup, seemed to sway slightly, a silent testament to his discontent.

The lack of genuinely good Earl Grey was also a concern. Reginald, bless his dusty little heart, was more of a Darjeeling man. And while Darjeeling had its moments, it simply couldn't match the robust, malty complexity of a perfectly brewed Earl Grey. He missed the sharp, citrusy notes, the subtle floral hints, the comforting warmth that only a superior Earl Grey could provide. The thought of spending eternity with only mediocre tea stung more than any misplaced wish ever had.

He pondered his current situation. He'd escaped the maddening demands of humanity, only to find himself grappling with the existential dread of lukewarm tea and subpar Darjeeling. Perhaps retirement wasn't all it was cracked up to be. Perhaps clause 3b of the genie contract hadn't been as forgiving as he initially thought. Perhaps a slightly-too-enthusiastic self-help guru was preferable to a lifetime of lukewarm tea.

A chipped mug, Beatrice, chuckled – a sound like tiny pebbles tumbling together. "Cheer up, old chap," she chirped. "There's always room for a little more sugar."

Azrael eyed her skeptically. "Sugar won't fix lukewarm tea," he grumbled, stirring his beverage with a miniature porcelain spoon. The spoon, it turned out, was surprisingly sturdy, a feature he appreciated. Small victories.

Fernando, ever dramatic, launched into a high-pitched aria about the plight of underappreciated espresso cups. His voice, though piercing, had a certain comforting familiarity. It was the kind of comforting noise that only exists in the bizarre world of mismatched teacups and lukewarm Darjeeling.

Azrael listened, a small smile creeping onto his face. Maybe, just maybe, retirement wasn't so bad. It was certainly different from what he'd envisioned, but perhaps that was the point. He'd swapped the tyranny of wish fulfillment for the tyranny of tepid tea. It wasn't exactly a grand exchange, but it was his, and at least he wasn't trapped in a teacup. And honestly, he had to admit the company was rather excellent, even if they did have a slightly concerning obsession with earthquake-proof ceramic craftsmanship. Perhaps the lukewarm tea wasn't so bad after all. Or perhaps, he simply lacked the energy to argue the point. It was, after all, a perfectly delightful retirement, if one could overlook the temperature of the beverage. Besides, there was always the possibility of finding a hidden stash of Earl Grey somewhere in this oddly charming, seismologically active dimension. He wouldn't give up hope just yet. The search, after all, would keep him occupied until the next earthquake. And perhaps, just perhaps, that's the kind of retirement a grumpy genie deserved. A grumpy, lukewarm, earthquake-prone retirement. A perfect, imperfect retirement. And honestly? He wouldn't have it any other way.

Acknowledgments

First and foremost, a heartfelt (yet slightly grumpy) thank you to my cat, Mittens, for providing endless inspiration – mostly in the form of hairballs and strategically placed obstacles on my writing desk. Without her constant, furry judgment, this book would likely still be a collection of half-formed sentences and existential dread.

Secondly, a nod of appreciation to all the hapless humans who, through their actions (and inactions), unknowingly contributed to the comedic chaos within these pages. Your unwitting participation is, frankly, remarkable.

Finally, a shout-out to my beta readers (you know who you are), who bravely endured the initial drafts and offered invaluable feedback, even when faced with Azrael's increasingly surly pronouncements. Your patience was truly magical. (And yes, I will eventually get around to fixing that plot hole you pointed out.)

Appendix

Clause 3b of the Standard Genie Contract (Excerpted): *Wishes shall be construed reasonably and within the bounds of both magical possibility and common sense. Excessively vague requests, demands exceeding the genie's capacity, or wishes solely for the purpose of annoying the genie shall be met with a resounding "No" and possibly a mild magical inconvenience. Excessive demands for "more wishes" will result in the immediate termination of the contract and a mildly passive-aggressive glare.*

Azrael's Personal Gripe List (Selected Highlights):
Teenagers.

Clueless magicians.

Forgetful librarians.

Reality TV.

Self-help gurus.

Sentient pigeons.

Teacups (especially small ones).
The inherent chaos of existence.

Glossary

Azrael: A genie of mildly grumpy disposition and considerably less magical power than advertised.

Clause 3b: See Appendix.

Sentient Pigeons: Pigeons with surprisingly advanced philosophical capabilities and a profound love of cheese.

Mild Magical Inconvenience: Anything from a small volcanic eruption to the summoning of an army of aggressively polite squirrels.

References

While this book is entirely fictional, the author readily admits to drawing inspiration from a multitude of sources, including but not limited to: bad days, overcaffeinated mornings, the endless stream of bizarre news headlines, and the general absurdity of modern life.

Specific titles are omitted to avoid accusations of plagiarism (or, frankly, embarrassment).

Author Biography

The author, a creature of indeterminate species and questionable sanity, spends their days battling writer's block (a surprisingly formidable foe), avoiding responsibility, and occasionally engaging in spontaneous interpretive dance. They reside in a location best described as "somewhere between reality and a particularly vivid daydream," and prefer to remain anonymous to avoid further interactions with overly enthusiastic fans (or disgruntled pigeons).

They may or may not own a cat. (Hint: See Acknowledgments).